DEMIGODS ACADEMY

YEAR TWO

ELISA S. AMORE
KIERA LEGEND

DEMIGODS ACADEMY

CHAPTER ONE

MELANY

*S*tunned, I stood frozen in the second row of the arena, staring at the God of the Underworld and wondering if all of this was an elaborate joke. Hades was known for his trickery and deception. Maybe this was his idea of a prank to pull on the most important day of the year for the academy. The most important day for the first year recruits. The most important day for me.

Hades looked beyond pleased with himself. He even had the nerve to wink at me, like I'd been in on the whole thing.

Chaos erupted around me. I didn't know what to do.

"You are not welcome here," Hera shouted at Hades.

"Ah, but sis, it's been too long. Aren't you happy to see me?" Hades gave a little bow, which just enraged her more.

"Where are the guards? Why aren't they here to apprehend him?" Hera asked of Zeus, but he looked just as confused as everyone else.

Revana stepped into the circle and pointed at me. "She cheated. Obviously, Hades helped her through the trials. She should be expelled for this and kicked out of the academy."

Of course she accused me of this stunt, anything to get rid of me. She couldn't stand I was just better than she was.

Others joined her in the cry that I had somehow cheated. They just looked for some lame excuse to implicate me in some nefarious plot. I wanted to yell at them that I didn't have anything to do with it, but I didn't think anyone would hear me. It was so loud in the arena with everyone talking at once, no one would listen to what I had to say.

While some of the Gods chose to be vocal about Hades's unexpected arrival, others attacked.

Ares waved his arms around in a panic. "Seize him!"

Armed with a sword, Heracles ran up on the platform and charged at Hades. Smiling, Hades waved his hand in the air, and a whip-like tendril of black smoke appeared and wrapped around Heracles's ankles, tripped him, and then hung him upside down over the platform. Heracles started shouting and cursing as he dangled over the cadets.

I pressed my lips together to stop from laughing; it was pretty funny.

Poseidon stepped out of the circle and created a huge cyclone of water around Hades. This started a panic among the recruits, who risked getting swept up into it. Screams echoed over the rush of water as recruits jumped down from the platform and fled toward the main door, which was still closed. Most of the other Gods got out of the way, too. Hermes hovered above the fray with his large, golden wings spread wide and powerful.

I saw Jasmine and Georgina running in that crowd, and I hurried down the rows of seats to meet them. Lucian had been on the other side of the stadium, so I didn't see where he went. But I couldn't get past the crush of other students who were all clamoring to get out.

The wall of water encircled Hades; I couldn't see him through the blue spray. Poseidon smiled as did Zeus, thinking they had captured their brother. They should've known better. Hades didn't have his fearsome reputation for nothing.

Fire flashed in the middle of the platform where Hades had been standing. Then the water just evaporated, and steam filled the arena like a giant sauna. I

felt the mist on my cheeks. Once that cleared, I saw
Hades standing there, the last remnants of flames
disappearing from his fingertips. He wasn't even wet.

"Really?" Hades shook his head, a wry grin on his
face. "Is that all you got? I expected more from you,
baby brother." He lifted his hands toward Poseidon, but
before he could do anything, Zeus clapped his hands
together. White sparks erupted from between them and
fell to the ground, sizzling the floor on impact. A crack
of thunder shook the whole building. I grabbed the
railing beside me, so I didn't fall over.

"ENOUGH!"

Silence filled the stadium, as the echoes of thunder
faded.

Hades let his hands drop to his sides with a disappointed sigh.

"Open the door and release the recruits." Zeus
nodded to Antiope and Achilles, who had been guarding
the door. "Please assemble in the dining hall and wait for
further instructions." The doors opened, and everyone
started to stream out. I pushed into the crowd to follow.
"Everyone may go but you, Miss Richmond."

My heart dropped into my gut. Of course. I locked
eyes with Jasmine; she gave me a horrified look, as she
was swept up in the crowd and out the door. Everyone
else went, too, until I was the only student remaining in
a room full of Gods and Demigods.

All eyes locked on me as I slowly made my way up

onto the platform. I didn't know where to stand. Next to Hades, because he claimed me? Next to Zeus, because he made the decision about my fate? I ended up standing by myself, on the edge of the platform, in case I needed a quick exit strategy.

Ares and Aphrodite continued to grumble about Hades appearance.

"I'm here. Deal with it." Hades glared at both of them. "And like I said before everyone had a hissy fit, I'm here to claim Melany for my own clan. She belongs to me. She's in my charge, and I will train her as I see fit."

"You can't just claim a recruit," Zeus said. "That's not how it works. A recruit must show signs that they belong to your——"

"She's beyond proficient with fire, is she not?" Hades raised an eyebrow at Hephaistos.

After a slight hesitation, Hephaistos nodded. "Yes. She is gifted, but——"

"She has produced black wings." Hades looked at Hermes, who still hovered in the air.

He floated down to the platform, golden wings folding in behind him. "Yes, and it is an anomaly, but doesn't necessarily mean——"

With no effort, huge black wings unfurled from Hades's back. He gave everyone a pointed look, and then his wings folded in again and disappeared.

"And she has a mastery of the shadows." His gaze

swept the stage and found Erebus, who had been almost hiding in the corner. "Come and tell them."

Erebus stepped onto the platform, swallowing. "Melany is very skilled in the shadow arts. She can manipulate the shadows to do her bidding. She can even tr... er..." He brought his hand up to cough, and then he started talking again. "She can use them as a p —" He coughed again. It was almost like he was choking.

I noticed Hades staring at him. Was he purposely stopping Erebus from saying something about me? If so, then why? What did he want kept secret about my abilities?

Every time he opened his mouth to talk about me, he started to cough, and then he spit up something onto the ground. At first it looked like small stones, but they were reddish. After he did it a few more times, everyone stepped away from him; I saw that they were pomegranate seeds.

"Anyway," Hades said, turning away from Erebus. The shadow master sucked in a greedy breath of air. "The point is she possesses all the attributes belonging to me and my clan."

"She can also manipulate water and earth and lightning." Demeter stepped up beside Hades.

Hades's smile was slow and lazy, but vicious. "Yes, and so can I, to some extent."

Zeus glanced at Poseidon, who appeared a bit concerned, then back to Hades. "You don't have a clan here. You're not part of the academy."

"Yeah, and whose fault is that? You wouldn't let me be part of this." He gestured to the arena. "Besides, it's not really yours, is it?"

Everyone on stage glanced nervously at each other.

What did he mean the academy wasn't theirs? That didn't make any sense. The Gods had been recruiting for the academy for more than one hundred years. As a society, we reestablished all the temples of worship around the world, so we could make offerings to the Gods for their favor. If that wasn't for them, for the academy, then who was it for?

Zeus stepped forward, grabbed Hades's arm, and pulled him a foot away from everyone. They bent their heads close together to talk. I strained my ears but couldn't hear what they said.

I glanced around, unsure of what to do, searching for an ally, but I wasn't sure I had one here. Demeter had helped me in the past, and she did seem to be arguing in my favor here, as had Dionysus in his own way. Hephaistos was certainly less grumpy toward me than the others, and had worked with me on my shield after regular forging class. Or maybe I'd been stupidly mistaken, and none of the Gods cared about what happened here, or what happened to any of us. Maybe we were just pawns in some ancient family squabble.

After another few minutes of awkward waiting, Zeus and Hades walked back over to where me and the others stood. Zeus's expression wore frustration, his brow deeply furrowed, while Hades beamed.

"Melany will be under Hades's tutelage. She will go to live in Hades Hall outside of the academy, and train with him in whatever skills he sees fit to benefit the army."

Poseidon shook his head. "This is a mistake."

Hera threw up her hands and walked away.

Ares and Aphrodite expressed the most outrage.

"There should be a discussion and a vote," Aphrodite said. "This isn't fair."

I was curious as to why they were so adamantly against the presence of Hades at the academy.

Demeter, Dionysus, and Hephaistos all shared concerned looks but didn't say anything. Apollo, Artemis, Athena, and Hermes just shook their heads.

"Do I get a say in this? Since it is the rest of my life," I finally said, my voice a bit shaky.

Everyone turned toward me. I saw looks of concern, whether for me or the situation I couldn't distinguish, and looks of disdain.

"No," Zeus and Hades said in unison.

Zeus addressed the others. "This matter is settled. There will be no more discussion about it. Not between you and definitely not with any of the recruits."

His gaze rested on me again, and I could feel the intensity of it right in my bones. "I trust we can expect discretion from you, Miss Richmond."

I nodded, although I knew I was going to have a

hard time not discussing it with my friends. The second I saw them, they were going to bombard me with a million questions. And honestly, I wouldn't have any answers. Something monumental definitely happened here, but I had no real idea what it was.

"Okay, we have a celebration to prepare for," Zeus said. "The recruits will be expecting their reward for completing their trials."

"Am I allowed to leave and join my friends?" I asked, scared of the answer.

"Of course. You earned a celebration." Zeus gestured toward the open door of the arena.

Before I stepped off the platform, I glanced at Hades. He waved his fingers at me in dismissal. "I'll see you later, Melany. We're going to have a grand time together."

I swallowed, as I wasn't so sure.

CHAPTER TWO

MELANY

$\mathscr{I}$ joined the others in the dining hall. All the recruits sat at the long wooden tables in groups, talking. They all fell silent the moment I passed through the tall double doors. Jasmine, Georgina, and Lucian rushed toward me, all talking at once.

"What the hell just happened?" Jasmine put her hands on her hips and gave me a look. "You didn't have anything to do with that, did you?"

I frowned at Jasmine, surprised and hurt she'd ask me something like that. "Of course not."

"Are you okay? Did they do something to you?" Georgina grabbed my hand; she looked like she was going to cry.

"I'm okay. I swear."

Lucian pulled me into his arms. "What did Zeus say? Surely, you won't have to go with Hades. The most logical place for you is in Zeus's clan. With me."

I drew back and gazed at my closest friends, wondering what all of this meant. Would we even see each other again? No one had been clear on exactly what happened to us after we were sorted into our clans. Maybe this was it. Our last goodbye.

"I, uh, I'm going to be training with Hades."

They all gaped at me as if I'd just grown a second head. Then the comments hit me like rapid fire and I felt attacked.

"You can't."

"Are you crazy?"

"There has to be another way."

I shook my head. Anger began to creep inside me at the implications that I had control over the situation. "I don't have a choice. Just like you guys don't. We are all stuck in the clan chosen for us."

Jasmine had the decency to look admonished for her earlier accusation. She sighed and reached for me to give me a hug. "I'm sorry if I came off as a bitch. I was just so scared for you. This is all so messed up."

I agreed it was messed up, but what could we do about it? This was our lives now. We survived our first year in the academy. This was what we signed up for. It was just that I hadn't expected Hades. No one did. He threw everything for a loop. And now, we were two years away from being active soldiers in the Gods Army. Maybe by then, I would have found out what happened to my town of Pecunia, to Sophie, and be able to exact my revenge with all the power of the Gods behind me.

"Look, I don't know what's going on, or what's going to happen to us in the future, but let's just go and enjoy the celebration together." What I didn't say was it might be the last time we were all together. By the troubled looks on their faces, they already knew that.

After another ten minutes or so of milling about in the dining hall, two ceremonial horns blew, echoing through the hall. Moments later a parade of champions marched in, led by Heracles and Hippolyta. Behind them were Achilles, Bellerophon, Antiope, Helen of Troy, Eros, Psyche, and a few others I didn't know or recognize. A buzz of excitement rippled through the room, and everyone got to their feet, watching and waiting in anticipation of what came next.

"Congratulations recruits," Heracles bellowed. "You have successfully completed your first year of training and have now achieved the rank of cadet."

A wave of clapping and cheering flowed through the room.

"Because of this great feat, you have been rewarded with a special position in one of the Gods' clans. You should be proud of this achievement. Not everyone who trains at the academy makes it through. You are the best of the elite selection of recruits." He beamed at us all. "Now it is time to celebrate."

More clapping and cheers. I didn't join in. I didn't feel rewarded, but like I was being punished. Others in the room gave me suspicious and cautious looks, like I was someone to be skeptical of, or even feared. I didn't like it. It made my stomach churn.

"We are here to escort you to your celebratory feast." Heracles gestured to the path that the champions made between them, and we all lined up. Some jostled for position to be at the front, but I, and my friends, including Mia, Ren, and Rosie, stayed back, so we were the last of the group to file out of the dining hall and into the main corridor.

As the procession wound its way through the stone corridors of the academy to the great hall, where even now I could hear the distant echoing thump of music, a rush of excitement circulated through the group. Jasmine and Georgina positively glowed with exhilaration. Lucian did, too. He walked with his head up, proud and jubilant about what he'd achieved. They all deserved to be praised, to feel triumphant in their achievements. I'd never want to take that away from them.

Despite my smiles and attempts at frivolity, I didn't share their eagerness and excitement for what was to come. I was filled with ominous dread.

There was something else, something nefarious, going on in the academy behind the scenes. I didn't know what it was, but I did know it revolved around Hades and his unexpected arrival... and around me.

When the front of the procession reached the towering double doors of the great hall, they slowly swung open, and golden light bathed us. Loud thunderous music swirled around us, so Dionysus must've been DJing again. One by one, in pairs, and in small groups, we entered the hall for our celebration.

Before I could enter, Heracles gently grabbed my arm and pulled me to the side, leaning down into my ear. "I just want you to know that I'm on your side. Others are as well. You have friends in the academy." Then as if remembering himself and where he was, he straightened and pushed me into the room. "Go have fun, cadet."

His words comforted me, as I stumbled into the great hall and caught up with Lucian and the others. We all paused for a moment, taking in the splendor of the gallery. Everything was gold and white and radiating with warm light. Hovering about six feet above us, like golden balloons, were candle filled lanterns immersing the room in a luxurious illumination. Tall gold vases of white flowers encircled each ivory pillar filling the air with a slightly sweet aroma. Long tables covered in gold cloth lined three walls and were stacked with every food imaginable. Roast chicken and duck, tiny sage stuffed partridges, roasted potatoes and root vegetables next to delicate pasta dishes. And the dessert table had its own chocolate fountain, which Diego was now shoving his face under. Students lined up, eager to fill up their plates.

Lucian glanced at me. "Hungry?"

"Oh, hell yes."

Laughing, we grabbed a fancy plate and got in line. After stacking our plates with mountains of food, we found seats at one of the round tables circumventing the dance floor and sat and shoveled food into our mouths. By the time my plate was empty, I didn't think I could move.

Jasmine patted her flat stomach. "I have a food belly."

I leaned in to peer at her washboard abs. "Where?" I poked her and she laughed.

It felt wonderful to sit with my friends and joke around after months of hard work, like we were just ordinary teenagers at spring formal, and not warriors training to one day risk our lives in war if needed. I soaked it all in knowing it wasn't going to last.

I looked over at the DJ platform where Dionysus had his turntables and sound system. His hair was spiked up every which way like a demented hedgehog, and he wore dark sunglasses and a black cape. He spotted me, grinned, and then grabbed the micro-phone. "This next song is for all the bad bitches out there."

Red laser lights cut through the air, rising from the

ground to the roof, as the music dropped the beat. It rolled over me like a technicolor wave. I jumped to my feet and grabbed Lucian's hand, pulling him with me out onto the dance floor. Jasmine and Mia held hands on the floor. Ren and Rosie, even Georgina, all joined in until we were one massive group, jumping and bouncing to the music like pogo sticks.

"Put your hands up!" Dionysus shouted as the beat, that one glorious beat, dropped like a rock in water, rippling out to the entire room.

I closed my eyes, losing myself in the music. I swayed and gyrated, Lucian matching me with every move. I draped my arms around his neck, his around my waist, and we danced together, in synch, the heat of our bodies mingling as one entity.

Sweat slicked my skin, and I was so hot I wanted to tear off my robe, but I refrained, considering I only had on my underwear underneath. When the muses had come to dress us before the ceremony, Clio and Thalia wouldn't let me wear a bra, claiming it would ruin the elegant lines of my robe. It didn't matter now I supposed, as I wasn't about to undress, anyway. But I did want alone time with Lucian. My body was burning up for him.

I grabbed his hand and pulled him off the dance-floor and toward the main doors. He didn't say anything, didn't question me. By the wicked look in his eyes, I figured he was thinking about the same thing.

We found a dark alcove away from the noise and

revelry of the celebration and embraced. His hands pressed against my bare back, sending a pleasant shiver over my skin, as he leaned down and kissed me. My sudden gasp emboldened him, and he moved his mouth over mine, tasting and teasing, making my heart thump so hard in my chest it was painful.

I dove my hands into the silky waves of his golden hair and hung on as he backed me up against the wall. His hands became bold and moved over my body, touching me gently. A slight caress along my hip made my belly flutter and then up to brush just under the swell of my breasts making me gasp again.

Breathing hard, Lucian pulled back and rested his forehead against mine. "I think we're nearing dangerous territory here. I don't want to do anything neither of us is ready for."

Should I tell him I was ready? That I was scared we wouldn't have any more time together, that this was it for us? That if we didn't indulge in each other, we'd never get another chance to do just that?

My heart raced so fast I couldn't catch my breath. I couldn't think beyond the way my body vibrated under his touch.

"I'm going to go get us some drinks." His voice was a bit ragged and rough.

I nodded, licking my lips; they still tingled from his kisses.

He pulled back, looked me in the eyes, then after a quick peck on the tip of my nose, he ventured out into the main corridor before heading back to the great hall. I stepped out of the alcove and casually paced around the area, trying to get my heart rate back to normal.

Leaning against the railing, I gazed down the huge staircase to the main foyer. It was dark down there, the only light radiating from one or two flickering lamps along the stone walls. I looked up at the glass dome ceiling. The moon was full, and its light seemed to beam right through me. It seemed to want to expose me for a fraud, or it could've been that was how it made me feel, as its light glared at me. I didn't know why I felt that way. I'd earned my place here in the academy. I'd passed every trial; I never cheated, despite the accusations from Revana and a few others. Still, that feeling lingered deep inside me. Uncomfortable, I stepped out of the moonlight and into the shadows.

The moment my foot touched the darkened floor, the shadows seemed to undulate playfully. Frowning, I watched as they moved across the white tile like wisps of black smoke to envelop my sandaled foot. I lifted my leg, and the tendrils clung to me like spider webs. A prickling sensation rushed over my body, and it made me feel cold and clammy.

I turned to walk away—to get away—but the shadows followed me. Now, they didn't seem so playful, but aggressive, purposeful. I kept walking, faster by the second, but I couldn't outrun the darkness. As I moved down the corridor toward the hall, I looked for firelight to step into, but each time I moved toward one of the lamps, the flames blew out, plunging me into even more darkness. I could see the golden glow of the great hall ahead, but I wasn't going to make it.

Running seemed pointless. I stopped and let the shadows swallow me up.

CHAPTER THREE

MELANY

I was pulled through the darkness, as if strings were fastened to my skin. It felt the same way as being sucked through the water portal to the academy, except decidedly more uncomfortable. My lungs didn't burn, but everything else seemed to. Eventually, the shadows dissipated around me, and I was left standing in a wide black stone corridor leading to several rooms, with high vaulted ceilings; there were four doors on each side.

It was dim in the hall. Firelight escaped from narrow slits in the juncture of the wall and floor and cast an eerie glow across the smooth black stone. I swung around in a circle, took note of the tall closed doors behind me, but I didn't recognize where I was. It was like no hall I'd ever been in.

"Hello?" My voice echoed off the walls.

I didn't expect an answer, so I jumped when I heard a deep male voice.

"I'm in the library. Last door on the right."

Cautious, I walked down the corridor to the last room on the right. It was the only one with an open door. I stepped into the room and hovered there in the doorway surveying my new surroundings. Two walls contained floor to ceiling shelves with meticulously organized books. Not one looked out of place. There were more books here than I'd ever seen in one spot. The other wall showcased several paintings—Renaissance paintings of old Greek myths. I'd seen some of them in books about the Gods.

At the far end of the room were a massive dark stone fireplace, fire crackling within, and two high-backed, decorative chairs sitting on either side, a mahogany round table by each. And Hades sat in one of those chairs, sipping red wine from a delicate wine-glass, looking equally at home and on display in his sharp purple suit.

He smiled when our gazes locked. "Welcome." He gestured to the other chair. "Please sit and join me for a drink to celebrate."

I slowly moved across the room toward him. "Did you bring me here?"

"Technically, I just sent the shadows. You walked through them."

"It was kind of hard not to considering they swarmed me."

He chuckled. "Yeah, my shadows can get a tad aggressive from time to time." He pointed to the big chair. "Sit. Drink. Relax."

I considered not sitting but realized that was childish and a waste of my anger at being kidnapped. I sank into the velvety cushioned chair. Beside me on the table, the wineglass magically filled with red wine as I watched.

I picked the glass up and peered into it suspiciously. I sniffed it.

Hades shook his head with amusement. "Do you really think I'd poison you? After all I've done to get you here?"

I took a tiny sip of wine, letting it linger on my tongue. I didn't normally enjoy red wine, but this was surprisingly sweet. "Where is here?"

"My hall, deep below the academy. This is where you'll live now. You'll have your own room with an en suite. The soaker tub is exquisite." He took a sip of his drink, watching me intently over the rim. "You will train with me to hone your skills. If you do everything I say, you could become the greatest warrior this army has ever seen." His lips twitched up in a sly, lopsided grin. "Besides me, of course."

"Of course." I smirked. "What makes you think I want to be some great warrior?"

"I've been watching you over the course of the year. You play to win, not to get some participation ribbon."

"How could you have been watching me? You were banned from the academy, or so the rumors said."

He shrugged. "I have my ways." There was a mischievous glint in his eyes.

The dark form outside of the portal. The whispers in the halls. The shadows that guided me. My dreams. He'd been there beside me from the moment I'd arrived at the academy. But why me? What was so special about me? I wasn't one hundred percent sure I wanted to know that answer, so I didn't ask. Although, I was sure he wouldn't tell me the truth anyway.

Hades intrigued me. But he also scared me. Because I felt drawn to him, and I didn't know why.

I set the glass on the table and got to my feet. "I want to go back to the party. I want to see my friends."

"There is no going back, Melany. That's not how it works anymore. You're in my charge now. You're my protégé."

That was what he said, but in my mind, I heard the words... *You're mine.*

Angry, I walked toward the door.

"Where are you going?" He sighed.

"I'm leaving."

"Okay, have fun with that."

Before I left, I glanced over my shoulder at him. He

was still in his chair, casually drinking his wine, looking as if he didn't have a care in the world.

I marched back down the corridor to the towering main doors. At first I thought they were made of a dark wood, but they, too, were carved from stone. I reached for the large metal knob expecting it to be locked, but it turned in my hand, and I slowly pushed it open. As I walked through, the doors suddenly swung shut behind me, and I was in another corridor, which looked eerily the same as the last one.

I walked along the stone floor, my footsteps echoing off the walls. I passed three doors on either side, all closed except for one. When I peered inside, I saw it was the library—the same library—and Hades still sat in the chair near the fireplace.

When he saw me, he raised his glass. "Ready to see your room yet?"

I turned and ran down the corridor this time, pushed open the doors, crossed the threshold, and ended right back in the same hallway. It was an unending loop.

Frustrated, I ran to the first closed door on my left. I tried the handle; it was locked. I went to the next door, also locked. The third door wasn't locked, and I opened it, walked in, and had stepped into the library again. I whirled around to see the bookshelves behind me and no door.

Hades frowned. "Done running around yet?"

"No." I marched out of the library and tried the

room next door. The door was locked. I banged on it, tried to push it open, but it wouldn't budge. The next door opened, and I walked in, popping out of the door across the hall back into the main corridor where it had all started.

I raised my hands into the air and screamed, "Are you freaking kidding me!"

When I was done, my throat dry and hoarse, I glanced up to see Hades strolling out of the library. "I'll show you to your room."

He crossed the corridor and approached the second closed door on the left side. It was one of the doors that had stayed locked when I'd tried it. He put his hand on the door handle and turned it. The door opened.

Of course it did. This was his world, and he was a God. And I was just some puppet he was playing with.

Flames in the wall sconces burst into life the second I followed him through and stepped into a huge suite dominated by a king-sized canopied bed, with indigo blue covers and pillows, and thick curtains tied up against the four tall posters. The stone walls had several paintings of what appeared to be fearsome beasts and pretty nymphs hung on them, and large, oval gilded mirrors with words etched on the glass. There was a navy settee and a cast iron table in one corner near the ornate hearth. In another corner near the closet was a dressing table with a large mirror and a decorative chair.

It was all very elegant and royal looking and gothic

in shape and style. I could picture all the furniture as part of Dracula's castle from a book I'd once read. I looked so out of place with my white and gold robe, tiara, and sandals.

Hades gestured to an arched opening in one wall. "This is the en suite."

Inside the room were the toilet, sink, a waterfall like shower, and a claw-footed soaker tub.

He pointed to the drawers and cupboards near the sink. "Everything you need is in there. Soaps and shampoo and oils for your bath. I think there might even be a bag full of rose petals if that's what you prefer. Anything you want, just ask."

Rose petals? What did he take me for? A pampered princess?

I drank it all in. The room was bigger than the one Callie had had at the Demos estate. Although everything was all dark and stone and medieval like, it was still just as luxurious. In my lifetime, I never thought I'd have such a room to call my own. I couldn't stop my smile as I gazed around.

Hades must've spied my grin because he appeared positively pleased with himself as he went to the closet door and pulled it open. The lamp hanging from the ceiling flared to life as we walked inside. I gaped at the rows of clothes hanging along one wall and the rows of shoes and boots along another. The other wall was one giant mirror.

"Now that you're part of my clan, you should dress

the part." He pulled a long plum-colored velvet dress off the rack and held it up for me. I ran my fingers over it; it was soft and subtle, and I noticed it had two slits in the skirt along the sides, so a girl could still perform a roundhouse kick. It was also in my exact size, as if it had been made specially just for me.

"It's pretty, but not really me."

He put it back, pulling something else off a hanger. "How about this?" He handed me a pair of black leather pants, also in my size, and a navy leather corset. Then he gestured to a long black leather duster. He flipped it open to show me the silky dark blue lining inside. There were skulls painted all along the fabric. "I think this would look good on you. You'd look kick-ass."

I gnawed on my bottom lip as I played my fingers over all the fine, expensive-looking clothes. "Why?"

"Why what?"

"Why all this?" I studied him. "Why me?"

He narrowed his eyes as he regarded me. "Because Melany, you have darkness running through your blood."

I winced. I didn't know what he meant. I wasn't a bad person. At least I didn't think I was.

"Darkness is not this bad thing as most people would have you believe. As the other Gods like to blather on about." He shook his head sadly. "Darkness is power and strength and stealth. With my help, you will be able to access that power and use it."

I frowned. I wasn't as thrilled as he was to know I had darkness inside me. All my life I'd been told I was different, an outcast. No matter how hard I tried, I knew I'd never be like Callie and her friends. Light didn't shine from inside me, as it seemed to shine from them.

Now, I supposed I knew why.

Was I born with this darkness inside of me? Did I get it from my parents?

Hades gestured for us to leave the closet. He walked to the table near the hearth and poured water into a glass. He carried it over to me. I took it gratefully, drinking it all down in a couple of swallows.

"I know this is a lot to take in."

"That's the understatement of the year."

He gave me a soft smile. "It's been a long, interesting day. I'm sure you're tired now."

I yawned. I was tired. It kind of snuck up on me all of a sudden. Now that adrenaline wasn't coursing through my bloodstream, I was crashing down hard.

"You will find sleeping clothes in the closet and everything else you need in those drawers." He walked over to the bed and pointed to a silk cord hanging from the ceiling. "If you need anything at all, at any time, just pull on this, and Charon will get it for you."

"Who's Charon?"

"My butler. He's a bit of a grump, so don't be put off by his gruff manner. It's just how he is. He says it's from serving me for over a millennia, but I think it's just his low vitamin D levels. He doesn't get much sun." He winked.

And I giggled. I felt a bit drowsy. Almost tipsy. I stared at the water glass in my hand.

He took it from me and led me to the bed. "Get some sleep. We'll talk in the morning. Then we'll start your training."

"What if I want to leave?" My tongue felt fat in my mouth, and I wondered if I was mumbling my words. "Can I just open those big doors and go back to the academy?"

He looked at me a long moment. "No. You can't leave. That was part of the deal Zeus and I arranged."

I couldn't keep myself upright any longer. I fell back against the huge mattress, my eyes curling shut. Before I completely drifted away, I felt Hades' hands as he positioned me on the bed and pulled the blanket up to my chin, tucking me in.

CHAPTER FOUR

LUCIAN

*a*ll I could think about as I walked back to the alcove with our drinks was how much I wanted to kiss Melany again. Her lips were so soft, her body so hot, especially in that toga. She'd probably kill me for saying it, but she looked like a Goddess with the gold eyeshadow and glitter on her cheeks. In my opinion, she was prettier than Aphrodite.

But when I returned to the alcove, Melany was gone. I wandered out into the main corridor to look for her.

"Blue?"

I glanced over the railing and down into the foyer. It was empty and dark, no indication anyone was down there. I checked in every corner and hiding spot but didn't find her sitting in the dark, waiting for me. I didn't think she'd go back to her dorm without telling me first. She knew, as we all did, this was likely our last night together for a while.

I made my way back into the great hall. Maybe she got bored waiting for me, and we'd missed each other coming and going.

After setting the drinks on a table, I headed over to the buffet to see if she was filling up another plate. Training as we did required a lot of calories, and that wasn't going to change any time soon. It was likely going to get a lot more strenuous now that we were in our respective clans.

She wasn't at the buffet, so I went to the dancefloor to see if she was dancing. I spotted Jasmine and Mia in the middle of the fray jumping up and down but didn't spy any blue hair in the crowd. I looked around and saw Georgina sitting at the table on the edge of the dance floor eating a large piece of chocolate cake. I approached her.

"Have you seen Mel?"

"No. I thought she was with you."

"She was. I left her out in the corridor to get us some drinks, and she was gone when I got back."

I didn't want to appear concerned. It was stupid to be worried in a place like this. We were all warriors in training, and I knew Melany could take care of herself and then some. But with Hades arrival in the academy and his claiming of Melany, everything no longer seemed safe and secure. I didn't know exactly what was going on, but it was clear Hades had a fixation with her. And I didn't like it.

Georgina stood. "I'll help you look for her. I'll go check our dorm room. Maybe she went back to change. I know she hated the robe she was wearing."

I nodded. "I'll ask Jasmine and Mia to be on the lookout for her, just in case." I went onto the dance floor to talk to them.

Jasmine took one look at my expression and frowned, leaning into my ear. "What's going on?"

"Have you see Mel?"

She shook her head. "Not since we were all on the floor together."

"She was waiting for me out in the main corridor near the stairs, but I can't find her."

"We'll look for her with you." Jasmine grabbed Mia's hand, and we moved off the floor.

Georgina and I went one way around the hall, Jasmine and Mia went the other way. My gaze swept the entire area, and I couldn't see her anywhere. Ren met up with us on the other side of the hall; he must've seen us doing the sweep.

"What's up?"

"Looking for Mel. She's missing."

"I haven't seen her." Ren grabbed Rosie as she walked by. "Have you seen Melany?"

Rosie shook her head. "No, not since we were all dancing."

Once we all met up again, we left the hall and made our way back to the girls' dorm. I didn't wait at the end of the hall like I normally would have, entering with Georgina to her room. It was dark when we got there, and when Georgina flicked on the light, we saw that Melany wasn't there, and all her stuff was gone. Panic swelled inside me. Had Hades already taken her?

"Are you sure her stuff is gone?"

She gestured to the empty closet on Melany's side of the room. "Oh yeah."

Jasmine lingered in the doorway. "What the hell does that mean? She wouldn't just leave. Not after all we've been through. Doesn't make sense."

"Well, we're all supposed to move to our clan halls by tomorrow," Georgina said. "Maybe she got moved early."

"Against her will, would be my guess." I ran a hand through my hair, concern making my guts clench. "She was less than happy to be forced into Hades clan."

"Where else would she go?" Jasmine asked. "Maybe she went somewhere to think."

"Let's try the maze."

Together, we left the academy and rounded the building to the hedge maze. The stone statues guarding the entrance appeared even more menacing than usual. Or it could've been the dread coursing through me.

Before we entered the dark maze, I created a small ball of fire in the palm of my hand to light our way. If Melany was here, that fireball would've been huge and bright. Her manipulation of fire was extraordinary. I'd even seen Hephaistos eye her with appreciation when she was creating something in the flames.

The maze was large, and it took us a bit to get through it, as the path had changed since I'd been through it last. When we reached the center and the gazebo, my dread increased as the strains of an acoustic guitar greeted us.

The four cauldrons around the gazebo were lit, the flames swaying to the music emanating from within. The orange glow created an unsettling display of light and dark over the stone pillars and roof of the gazebo. Shadows created by the flames seemed to dance in celebration.

I wasn't surprised to see Hades sitting on the stone bench strumming his guitar when I took the three steps up into the gazebo. Jasmine, Mia, Georgina, Ren, and Rosie all lined up behind me. When he saw us, he smiled, but kept playing his song with a bit more gusto.

"Where is she?"

His gaze fixed on me; it looked like there were flames crackling in his eyes, but it must've been the reflection of the fire in the cauldrons. He smacked his hand down on the strings of the guitar, letting go one last twang.

"Where is who? I think you should be a bit more specific."

I took a step toward him. "Don't play games with me, Hades. I know you did something to Melany."

He set his guitar aside onto the bench beside him and leaned back against the railing, as if he didn't have a care in the world. He grinned again, and it was cold and calculating and sent an icy shiver down my back. "Haven't you heard, boy, play time is over?"

I took another step forward.

"Lucian," Ren warned from behind me.

"Where is Melany?! What did you do to her?!" I demanded.

"What makes you think I'd do anything to her? She's my protégé now. She's special. Very special." He ran his fingers across his mouth. "But you obviously already know that about her."

He dripped with arrogance, and it got my blood up. Heat swelled in my hands, then sparks. Ropes of lightning encircled my fingers. One flick of my wrist and I could send a few bolts toward Hades. But before I could do anything drastic and stupid, Ren, Jasmine, and Georgina all grabbed me and kept me from charging toward the dark God. They probably saved my life.

Chuckling, Hades stood. He brushed at his pants and adjusted his shirt collar. "I admire your courage, Lucian. And it appears you have some ability." He lifted his hands and wiggled his fingers. Electrical sparks coiled around his hands, but it wasn't white lightning; it was as black as ink. "My brother must be pumped to have you in his clan."

I quickly snapped my hands closed, cutting off the

flow of current. I sagged back against my friends, knowing I was foolish to think I could ever hope to go against a God as powerful as Hades.

"I understand your desire to fight me, Lucian. I like it. Shows great spunk." Hades shook his hands out, and black sparks bounced onto the ground then fizzled. "And Melany… is definitely worth fighting for."

He licked his lips, as if he was thinking about the most delicious meal he was set to devour.

I broke free of my friends' hands and rushed at him, my fists up to fight.

With a snap of his fingers, Hades dissolved into tendrils of black smoke, which swirled up into a dark tornado, blowing back my hair. Then the smoke vanished into thin air. All that remained was his acoustic guitar.

I picked it up and smashed it into a hundred pieces. It didn't do much to satisfy the rage coursing through me like wildfire.

"Lucian, stop!" Jasmine came to my side. She didn't touch me though, which was probably best.

Breathing hard, I sagged against the side of the gazebo. "He has her, Jasmine."

"I know. It'll be okay. Mel's tough. She can handle herself."

I nodded, but I wasn't so sure. Physically, I knew Melany could handle anything anyone threw at her, but I wasn't worried about Hades pushing her physical limits. I was worried he held some kind of mental thrall over her. I remembered how she'd sounded when she talked about Hades, about seeing him here in the gazebo, playing his guitar for her.

She sounded intrigued by him. Melany was a curious person, and it scared me to think what she'd do to satisfy that curiosity.

CHAPTER FIVE

MELANY

a sudden clanging sounded near my ear jolting me out of sleep. I blinked open my eyes to stare at the black canopy over top, trying to establish where the hell I was. I turned my head to see more dark things—the pillows, the blanket, the drapes clinging to the canopy, the round table near the bed. Then it came back in a heady rush, and I rolled over onto my side as nausea washed over me.

I was in Hades Hall with Hades.

But what the hell was that clanging noise?

Slowly, I sat up and stretched. That's when I spied the bell hanging on the wall near the canopy. It rattled back and forth setting my teeth on edge. Obviously, it was my new alarm clock.

I stretched again and stood. The bell kept ringing. "Argh. Okay, I'm up. Jeeze."

Instantly, the bell stopped. Well, that was creepy.

When I took a step forward toward the bathroom, something moved in the shadows in the corner near the closed door. I held my breath as a tall form in a hooded robe floated toward me. I clenched my hands, flames immediately engulfing them, and then raised them, ready to attack.

The form stopped, lifted long, bony hands, and drew back the hood to reveal a skeletal face, large rheumy eyes, and brown rotten teeth showing between pulled back thin, wrinkled lips. His long, white beard hung in a scraggly mess down his chest.

I screamed. I couldn't help it. It was a reflex.

"Good morning, miss." His voice was as brittle as yellowed old paper. "I hope you slept well."

Breathing hard with my heart hammering in my throat, I didn't lower my hands. "Who are you?"

"Charon, miss. Lord Hades has instructed me to inform you that breakfast will be served in the dining room promptly at seven and not to be late. Also, your training clothes are hanging in your closet."

Slowly, I lowered my hands and extinguished the flames sparking between my fingers. "Please tell me, Charon, that you're not going to be in my room every morning."

"Of course not, miss. That would be rude." He bowed his head then turned and floated toward the door, which opened on its own, and he sailed through, and the door shut behind him.

Once he was gone, I went into the bathroom, washed, and then went into the closet to get dressed. My training clothes consisted of black leggings and a long-sleeved, tight shirt, in a material that felt both lightweight and heavy. Almost like armor but without any bulk. I put on the black boots accompanying them.

I came out of my room, glanced around, and had no idea where the dining room was, so I checked all the doors. Two doors were locked, and when I tried the third, it opened into a large dining room, dominated by a long mahogany table with only two chairs, one at each end. Hades, dressed all in black, sat at the far end, sipping from a tea cup. There was another place setting of tea at the other chair.

"Good morning. You're on time. Good. Sit." He gestured to the end of the table. "Breakfast will be served shortly."

I sat and looked into the cup in front of me. I sniffed it, wrinkling my nose. Smelled gross.

"Drink it. It's good for you."

I met his gaze across the table, pissed. "Oh, like the water you drugged me with was good for me last night?"

He waved his hand at me. "I didn't drug you, Melany. You were tired; it had been a very long and stressful day. Even for me. Fighting with my brothers always wears me out. I zonked out the minute my head hit my pillow."

"Your butler scared the crap out of me this morning in my room. Does he always creep around?"

"Yes, I'm afraid that's his default state of being." Hades chuckled. "I'll make sure he doesn't pop in on you like that again. I think he was just excited to meet you. I haven't taken on a... recruit in a very long time."

"You used to teach here?"

"Don't look so surprised." His face scrunched up. "I'm a pretty decent teacher. I used to get all the apples." His grin was quick and sly and did funny things to my belly.

I swallowed, feeling a bit warmer than before. "Why were you banned from the academy?"

"It's a long story, and one you don't need to know right now."

The door behind Hades swung open and one of Hephaistos's little serving robots wheeled out with two plates of hot food. It stopped beside Hades and handed him a plate, then wheeled down to me. I took the plate of eggs, toast, sausage, and potatoes and set it down on the table in front of me. Then the little robot zoomed back through the door.

"Does Hephaistos know you have one of his robots?"

"Of course. He and I have an understanding. Now eat. You're going to have a long day of training, and you're going to need the energy."

After we ate, I followed Hades down the corridor to the closed door next to the library. Last time I checked, the door had been locked, but it naturally opened to Hades. I followed him in and was stunned. Of course every room in Hades Hall defied the laws of physics and form, and this room, although it seemed silly to call it merely that, was a glaring testament to the deception.

It was as spacious as the training studio in the academy and reminded me a bit of a martial arts dojo, as one wall was covered in an array of weapons, from Bo staffs to long bows to ornate curved daggers. Close to that wall was a row of wooden training dummies. And across the room on the far side was an obstacle course, with hanging ropes to climb, narrow beams to walk, razor wire to crawl under, and a cement wall to scale.

Several tall torches lit the room, situated every few feet along the walls. It felt like we were in some ancient gladiator arena.

Hades spread his arms, gesturing to the room. "This is where you will train every day."

I walked to the weapon wall and ran my fingers over one of the broadsword's blade. I'd had some training with a few of the weapons on the wall, but not all of them, and I was eager to give them a try.

I spun around and looked him up and down. "And you're going to train me?"

His eyebrow arched. "Yes, in some of the combat tactics." He snatched a couple of the knives on the wall. One in each hand, he spun them around flaw-lessly, fluidly, and then with a flick of his wrists, they zipped across the room. One impaled a wooden dummy right in the middle, and the other dagger hit the next one in the same spot. It was impressive.

"But most of your training will be with my associates." There was a sly smile on his face as he looked up at the ceiling.

I followed his gaze and spotted three large forms moving about in the shadows on a ledge twenty-five feet above us. Then one by one, they swooped down and landed next to Hades. Their appearance startled me, and I took a few unsteady steps backward. I'd thought Medusa and Chiron had been unsettling to interact with.

But these creatures took things to a whole new level. I'd read about the Furies in a book about the Gods. They embodied anger, vengeance, and jealousy. The very air changed the moment they arrived. It was a chaotic energy, and it made the hairs on my arms and the back of my neck rise.

"Welcome ladies." Hades gestured to the first new arrival on his left, who towered over him. "This is Allecto."

She had long, bright red hair braided in two lines, one on each side of her angular face. Blood red eyes glared down at me, crimson lines running in tear stains down her face. Between her full, pale lips, I could see tiny, razor-sharp kitten teeth that looked more deadly than cute. Massive black leathery wings loomed behind her, the ends of them hooked much like those of a bat. Other than those oddities, she resembled a regular woman, except extremely muscular and tall. She would've loomed over Hippolyta.

"And this is Tisiphone and Megaera."

Beside Allecto stood her sister. I assumed it was as they shared the same facial features, but she had short, raven black hair. She also had red eyes with streaks of blood staining her cheeks, tiny fangs, and similar large, black wings. Although she wasn't as tall or as bulky, she was still intimidating and fierce looking, and she studied me like she wanted to dine on my blood and bones.

Next to her was a slighter, shorter woman; she was only a couple of inches taller than me, with long, stringy green hair. She shared all the same physical features, though, as her sisters. Her gaze was more pointed when she looked me up and down.

She smirked. "This is who you've chosen?" Her voice was high-pitched and shrill, making me shudder.

"She's tougher than she looks."

"She better be, or we'll break her within minutes of training." Allecto leaned down to scrutinize me. She sniffed the air around me and then snarled, "She reeks of fear."

I swallowed, taking a step forward. "I'm not afraid."

Although I was shaking inside, I wasn't going to let

them intimidate me. I didn't go through hell in the twelve trials to be bullied around by three bat girls.

Tisiphone grinned, her teeth gnashing. "Yeah, we'll see about that."

Hades patted her on the shoulder. "Be nice, Tis. I need her to stay in one piece, okay?"

"I'll think about it." She sniffed and then flexed her wings. The hooked ends came very close to my face. Allecto and Megaera snorted and chuckled.

I couldn't let them push me around, especially since I was going to be training with them every day. I had to show them I wasn't scared, although I was a little, and that I wasn't someone to mess around with.

Puffing out my chest, I focused my mind. Seconds later, my black feathery wings split through my shoulder blades and unfurled around me, twelve feet of wingspan. All three sisters' eyes widened in surprise.

Hades chuckled. "There's the fierce girl I saw in the trials."

Megaera sneered. "Fierce? We'll see about that."

Tisiphone bent toward me, reaching out to touch the tip of my wings. She pulled a face. "Not bad. They look good. Can you use them?"

Without hesitation, I shot up into the air, flapping once to gain velocity. I flew up to the ceiling, touched the crossbeams, and then swooped over to the ropes hanging down. I grabbed one and swung myself around, then let go, and flew off like a shot again to the other side of the training studio.

Laughing, Tisiphone clapped, cheering me on.

Hades's grin was instant and huge, and I felt a sort of pride swell in my heart.

Allecto just sneered.

Not to be out done, Megaera took to the air with a loud whoosh of her wings. As I hovered near the corner of the studio, she flew right at me. Folding my wings in, I dropped, then right before I reached the ground, I released them and soared just over Hades and the others' heads. I caught Hades's pleased chuckle as I swooped overhead.

Megaera came at me again, arms outstretched. I was about to dodge her and turn right, when two green whips snapped out of her wrists. The tips just brushed the top of my head, and it was then I realized, with sickening dread, that the whips were snakes. I heard their hiss as their open mouths snapped right by my face.

Shocked, my wings folded into my body, and I dropped like a sack of rocks to the floor. Before I could break my limbs in the fall, Hades caught me in his arms, and then set me back onto my feet. I wobbled a little but I didn't fall.

I couldn't believe what I just saw. I gaped at Megaera as she landed softly next to her red-headed sister. She rubbed at her wrists, and I saw painful looking red slashes across her skin where the snakes had broken through.

"There, I knew you'd all get along. Just like one big,

happy family." Hades clapped his hands gleefully. He patted me on the shoulder. "Have fun. I'll leave you to your training. I'll see you at dinner."

Then he left the room, leaving me with three very strange and very unpleasant women, who I suspected had no intention of seeing me succeed.

CHAPTER SIX

MELANY

"*Y*our flying's not bad." Tisiphone folded her wings behind her back. They didn't retreat into her body like mine had. "But we will teach you to be even better."

Megaera snorted. "She flies like a tiny chick."

"Now, now sister, don't be so harsh on the poor girl. She just got her wings while you've had yours for over a thousand years." Tisiphone patted her sister on top of her green head like a child.

Megaera batted her hand away. "Whatever."

"Stop bickering," Allecto snarled at her sisters then glared at me. "Are you ready to start training?"

I nodded. "Yes."

"Good." She walked toward the weapons wall. I

rushed to her side to join her. "In combat you must be able to pick up any weapon and know how to kill with it."

I flinched at her bluntness, but the truth was I was a soldier training in an army. I not only needed to know how to defend myself and others, but how to kill. If someone or something was coming at me or those I loved, I couldn't hesitate to act.

She plucked a large mace with a spiked ball at the tip from the wall and handled it like it was made of plastic and not iron. She made her way to one of the wooden combat dummies, the one Hades had impaled with a knife, and swung the mace overhead. It came down on the dummy and broke it into pieces. With one mighty blow, she had demolished it, reducing it to toothpicks.

Turning her fierce gaze on me, she tossed me the mace. I caught it with both hands. It was heavy, but I'd been holding a sword for months now, so my muscles didn't shake.

She pointed to the other wooden dummy. "Let's see what you're made of."

"Won't Hades be angry we're breaking his things?"

Allecto's brow furrowed. "Do you really care?"

I couldn't stop the grin spreading across my face. "Nope." I hefted the mace over my head and brought it down. The wood cracked, one of the pegs broke off, but that was it. Despite the limited damage I'd inflicted, it still felt good.

She sucked on her teeth, looking at me with thinly veiled distaste. "You have some bulking up to do, so that next time you wield that mace, it will be lethal."

For the next seven hours, I trained harder than I ever had before. The three sisters put me through my paces challenging me at every turn.

Under Allecto's drill sergeant-like instruction, I did fifteen pullups on the metal bar (she wanted me to do fifty) thirty-five pushups (she expected one hundred), and then I had to run the obstacle course five times in a row. During the last run, I got a cut on my cheek from the barbed wire I had to crawl under, and I couldn't get over the cement wall. In fact I had a hard time holding my arms up, so I sort of shuffled around it, my arms hanging uselessly at my sides.

Tisiphone and Megaera had been on the sidelines, cheering and jeering me on, respectively.

"Yeah, you did it!"

"I've seen baby centaurs do better than you."

After a short break where I gulped down at least half a gallon of water and tended to my small cut, which I cleaned and dressed with a bandage—I had been shocked they had a first aid kit available in the room—I was handed off to Megaera for flying lessons.

"Unfurl your wings," she demanded roughly.

Concentrating hard, I pushed my wings out through my shoulder blades and spread them out wide around me.

"That took too long. In a combat situation, you'd be dead already."

"It was like a few seconds."

"A few seconds is all it takes for an arrow to pierce your eye." She thrust her fingers toward my eye. "Or Medusa to turn you to stone or one of my snakes to bite your throat and inject you with lethal poison." She rubbed her wrist when she said this, and I wondered if she was fantasizing about just that. "In combat your wings should already be out."

"You want me to fight while I'm winged?"

"Yes. Makes you ready for anything."

"But they're so heavy. I'm not sure I—"

She punched me in the chest. I staggered back a step. "This is why you need to get stronger. Your chest, shoulders, and back muscles need to be like steel."

I nodded.

"Now, fold your wings back."

Using my back muscles, I pulled my wings in as tight as I could. I had a sense they still stuck out. Megaera came around behind me, poking and prodding at my wings.

She folded them even more than I could. "There, that will do for now." She came back around in front of me. "We're going to practice taking off mid run. In combat you could be exchanging sword volleys in one second and flying the next to attack another opponent. Watch me."

She nodded to Tisiphone. "Toss me a sword."

Tisiphone snatched a short sword off the wall and threw it to Megaera. She caught it, spun it once around with her wrist, thrust it out, and then started to run. After a few long strides, she launched into the air, and flew across the room in a few seconds. Then she swooped down and landed lightly in front of me again.

"You try." Megaera handed me the sword.

I held it up and sprinted across the room, stopping to spring into the air, my wings unfurling and flapping hard. I had only risen a few feet when she shouted at me to land.

She shook her head. "Horrible. You'd be dead by the time you got into the air."

"According to you, I'm going to die just by walking around." I smirked.

She didn't appreciate my humor and glowered at me with blood red eyes, which sent a shudder down my back.

"You could die right now…" She lifted a hand.

"Meg," Tisiphone warned. "Play nice. Hades has entrusted us with Melany's care. You don't want to disappoint him, do you?"

Megaera sighed and lowered her hand. "Whatever." She came to stand beside me, grabbing me around the hips. "When you are running, don't stop. Instead, bend your knees and tilt your pelvis. It will help you get power to launch into flight." She released me and then stood back. "Try it again."

Taking in a few quick breaths, I lifted the sword and

ran full tilt across the room. I did what she said and
bent my knees midstride, but I ended up tripping over
my feet and falling face first onto the floor. Thank
Gods, I had the forethought to thrust my sword to the
side, or I would've fallen on it.

I heard someone laughing. I assumed it was Tisiphone, as she seemed like the only one who had a sense
of humor.

"Get up. Do it again."

I did.

I fell two more times. On the third try, I stopped
and jumped again. The fourth try I got off the ground,
but my wings didn't unfurl in time, and I just fell back
down. On the fifth try, I ran as hard as I could and
sprang midstride, going air born. I flapped up and
soared across the room, the tips of my wings brushing
the ceiling arrogantly.

When I came back and landed near Megaera, she
didn't smile, but she did nod. "Not bad."

Tisiphone smacked her sister on the back. "Pretty
high praise from this one."

I tried to hide my smile, as I didn't want to draw
Megaera's wrath again. Out of the three sisters, she
was the one I worried most about. Not that I trusted
any of them, but Megaera seemed like she'd have no
trouble literally stabbing me in the back. I had a feeling
she'd take great pleasure in it.

After another quick break, I started my stealth
training with Tisiphone.

"I know you know how to use the shadows to cloak yourself and to move around. But to be truly invisible, you need to learn how to move around in darkness. Complete darkness without any sound." She smiled, and every torch in the room extinguished, and we were plunged into blackness.

I didn't know what to do, or what she wanted me to do, so I stood as still as possible and tried to control my breathing. Then a tap came on my right shoulder, and I spun that way, then a tap on my left, and I spun back around. I hadn't heard her move. There were no footsteps, no rustling of clothing or shoes. Mind you, the sisters didn't wear shoes.

"I am five feet behind you. Come and find me." Her voice startled me and I flinched.

"I can't see, so how can I?"

"Focus on other things beside what you can see with your eyes. Concentrate on what you hear. What you can smell. The movement of the air on your skin."

I obeyed and focused on the direction her voice had come from. I took a hesitant step forward, stopped, listened, and then took another step forward. I tried to stop my heart from thundering in my ears, so I could zero in on other sounds in the room.

There. I heard the slight crinkle, like paper moving, of Tisiphone's wings shifting. I course corrected and took another step forward. I stopped, frowning, lifting my arm up to see if I could feel a shift in the air. For a moment, I only felt my own puffs of breath as they stirred the hair on my arms. Then I felt something else. A whoosh of movement. Something approached my right side.

I whirled around. The flames sparked, and I was face to face with Tisiphone. She had her dagger's tip nearly pressed into my side.

She grinned. "Good job. I almost had you."

I knew she'd pulled back deliberately. She could've slid that knife between my ribs any time she wanted to. I appreciated that she didn't.

"Now, I'll teach you how to walk without making a noise. Right now, you slap your foot down with every step you take. I could hear you from a mile away."

For the next hour, Tisiphone showed me how to walk on the outer edge of my feet. Then she threw down gravel over the floor and made me walk across it. Every time I made a sound, she threw one of those small pebbles at me. By the time I was done for the day, my body felt like it had been stoned.

When my training was done, they all informed me we'd be doing it all over again tomorrow. And the next day and the next, and that I should probably have a long, hot soak in the bath with some salts for aches and pains. Tisiphone informed me there should be a small bag of special salts in my bathroom, brewed by Dionysus.

I walked across the corridor and to my room. My legs and arms ached with every movement. A hot bath sounded glorious. When I entered my room, I found a long, sleeveless velvet black dress fanned out on my bed, beneath it on the floor was a pair of black heels. On the dress was a note:

Spend the next two hours in the bath and resting, then put on this dress and meet me in the dining hall for dinner. Hades

I picked up the dress; it was pretty and elegant, and so not something I would ever wear. I wondered how angry he'd be when I showed up for dinner in leather pants and a T-shirt instead. I set the dress down and padded into the bathroom to start my bath. I guess I was going to find out, because there was no way I was wandering around in that dress for anyone.

CHAPTER SEVEN

MELANY

I stayed in the bath until the water turned cold. I didn't know how long I stayed, as there wasn't a clock in the room, and I didn't have my cell phone, but it felt like hours. I grabbed the fluffy black robe that had been left for me in the bathroom, put it on, and wandered into the closet to get dressed for dinner.

The lamp automatically flared to life when I walked in—that was going to take some getting used to—and I immediately saw the closet was empty. Lonely hangers swung back and forth on the rod, and after I rushed to the drawers and pulled them open, I discovered there weren't any clothes folded neatly in there, either.

"What the hell?" I murmured.

I went back into the bedroom, my gaze focused on the dress still spread out on the bed. When I neared it, I saw another note on the dress.

You will wear this dress tonight for dinner like I'd asked. Hades

Pissed, I crumpled up the note in my hand, and lit it on fire, until there were only bits of ash left in my palm. I opened my hand and let the ash float to the floor. I was uncaring if it made everything dusty and dirty. I shook my head. I couldn't believe he'd removed, or gotten Charon to do it, all my other clothes just so I'd wear this dress. How did he know I wasn't going to wear it? Was he spying on me? Did he hear my thoughts? Gods, they thought they could control everything.

I shuddered thinking about that possibility.

Without any other option, except for the robe I wore, I picked up the dress and put it on. There was a full-length mirror near the dressing table in the room, and I stood in front of it. I hated that the dress fit perfectly and accentuated my defined shoulders and arms and pale skin, along with exposing a healthy length of leg. I didn't want to consider what the plunging neckline did to my breasts, but the fact was I looked hot in this dress.

I did a spin, then a round house kick with my right leg, executing it flawlessly. I looked at myself in the mirror again.

Damn it. I also looked bad ass in this dress.

After doing my hair—I mean I had to because I was wearing this great dress—and putting on a little lip gloss I'd found in a drawer in the bathroom, I made my way down the corridor to the dining room.

I opened the door to find the room lit by a bunch of tall candles on the table, and our meal already laid out. It smelled delicious and my stomach rumbled in response. Hades walked toward me, an unreadable look on his face as he gazed at me.

He gave me a little bow. "You look beautiful."

His compliment pleased me, and I felt my cheeks flush a little under his searching gaze. "Thank you."

"I knew the dress would look extraordinary on you."

"Well, you didn't really give me a choice. Cool trick making all my clothes vanish."

His smile came quickly. Again, my belly flipped a little over it. "I suspected you were going to come in a pair of jeans and T-shirt if given half the chance."

"Leather pants actually. Since there aren't any jeans in the closet."

He pulled out the chair for me to sit. "Jeans are for lazy people. And you are far from that."

I sat in the chair, and he pushed it up for me, and then he picked up a bottle of wine that had been chilling in a metal bucket of ice. He poured some into my wine glass, took it back to his side of the table, filled his glass, and then he sat.

He lifted his wine glass. "To the first day of a new chapter for the both of us."

Although I wasn't sure he was just talking about my training in his clan, I took up the glass and drank. The wine was sweet and delicious and surprisingly refreshing, something I desperately desired after the hard day of training. I took another sip before setting my glass down and digging into my food. I was starving.

As I shoveled food in my mouth, I sensed that he was watching me from across the table. I glanced up to see an impish lift of his mouth. "What? I'm hungry."

"I take it my assistants pushed you hard in your training."

"That's putting it mildly."

"Nothing you couldn't handle, I'm sure."

"I'm pretty sure Megaera would put a knife in my back if given half the chance."

He shrugged, taking a sip of wine. "Probably."

I set my fork down and wiped my mouth with the fancy linen napkin. "Why am I here?"

"To eat, obviously."

"No, why am I *here*?"

"To train for the Gods Army, to defend the world from—"

"This would all be a lot easier if you'd just be honest with me."

Amused, he leaned back in his chair. "That's why. Because you don't buy into all the bullshit. You're inquisitive, brash, and stubborn, to a fault quite possibly, but we'll see about that... Anyway, I like that you question things."

"Even you?"

His grin got bigger and predatory, and I swallowed, suddenly nervous. "Especially me. Makes it way more fun to have you around. I love a challenge. I've been so bored lately."

"I'm so happy I'm amusing you." Anger swelled inside me. It burned as if my organs were on fire. I didn't want to be a prisoner here. That was exactly how I felt, and Hades was the warden. I stood, pushing the chair back with force. It nearly toppled over. "I'm not your play thing. You can't just dress me up and parade me around like I'm some doll."

"Are you finished having your temper tantrum? Can we continue on like adults?"

I whirled around and marched toward the door.

"I guess not." His voice followed me out of the room.

I clenched my fists. I hated his condescending attitude. I wasn't going to put up with it. I stomped down the corridor and back to my room. Slamming the door shut, I dragged one of the big, heavy chairs that stood near the hearth across the floor and jammed it up against the door handle. I knew if Hades wanted in, a stupid chair wasn't going to stop him, but it was the principle of the action that mattered.

I paced my room, so angry I couldn't sit still. I didn't like this situation. It wasn't normal, although at this point, normal didn't have the same connotation it had a year ago. I wanted to be with my friends. I missed them. They were probably worried about me, or at least I hoped they were. Lucian probably thought I had just up and left him without a word. It wasn't right.

I stomped into the closet. I wasn't going to wear this dress any longer. I didn't care if I didn't have anything else to wear. I'd go naked if I had to, but when I entered and the lamp flared, I saw that my entire wardrobe had conveniently returned.

After stripping off the dress, I put on a pair of leather pants and long-sleeved black shirt. I knew it was late, although I didn't know exactly what time it was, but I had no intention of putting on pajamas and going to bed like an obedient child. Screw the rules. I was going to find a way to get the hell out of here. Once I was out, I would beg Zeus to take me into his clan. Surely, passing all the trials for the first time in history gave me some kind of upper hand, or what was the freaking point?

I paced my room some more, waiting. I wasn't sure what I waited for. For Hades to go to sleep? Did the God even do something as mundane and human as that? All I knew was it felt right to wait. I did some jumping jacks and crunches to stay alert. I splashed water on my face to keep awake.

Finally, after I estimated two hours had passed, I decided to make my escape.

I pushed the chair away from the door, then opened

it, and peered out. The corridor was empty and mostly dark except for the firelight emanating from the slats in the wall. I crept out, walking on the sides of my feet like Tisiphone had taught me. When I reached the closed main doors, I knew opening them and going through was pointless. I was just going to end up right back where I started.

But I knew another way to travel.

Because there was light nearby, there were also shadows. One didn't exist without the other. I stepped into one, concentrating on drawing the darkness to me. At first nothing happened, but then I could see the murkiness slowly draw along the floor and envelop my boots. I coaxed it up my legs and over my torso, until I was completely swallowed up by it.

Like before when I'd used the shadows to sneak up on Medusa during the twelfth trial, my body felt like it floated in salt water. I raised my hand, my arm weight-less, and looked at it. It was attached to my body, but I didn't feel it. It was a strange sensation.

Concentrating on what I needed to do, I took a step forward in the darkness. It was like walking on air, there was no form and substance under my foot, or at least none I could sense. I took another step, then another. Back in the corridor, I would've walked right into the doors by now, but this shadowy world wasn't corporeal.

I kept walking, sensing I had bypassed Hades's looping trick, and headed in the right direction. After a few more steps, I felt a denseness under my boots. I was walking on something hard. A spot of light formed in the distance, and I moved toward it.

Another three steps and I emerged from the shadows. I felt the darkness fall away, like a snake shedding its skin. I looked around to get my bearings. Large, greenish rock masses hung down from a ceiling I couldn't see; it was too far up. More formations jutted out from the ground. I was in a huge cave, much like the one that had been at the end of the portal to the academy.

The air held the scent of water; it was also cool against my skin. Was I near the ocean again? Was this how I was going to get back to the academy? Was I going to need to swim? Maybe Hades Hall hadn't been under the academy like Hades had told me. It wouldn't have surprised me if he'd lied about that.

As I walked farther along the rugged and uneven rock floor, I could hear the rushing of water nearby. When I crested a slight slope, I saw it. It wasn't an ocean but a river flowing through the cavern. As I approached, I spotted a thick mist rolling over top of the water. Moonlight seemed to reflect off the surface, giving it an eerie glow, but when I looked up, I couldn't see any moon.

Okay, I just had to cross this. It was no big deal. I had the ability to manipulate water, and I could hold my breath for a long time. I wasn't an expert at it, not like Ren, but I had passed the trial easily enough, despite the attack of the hydra and nearly drowning in the waves it made.

Standing on the shore with the water lapping at the toe of my boot, I raised my hands over the river and concentrated on moving it. I wondered if I could part it like Moses had done in the Christian fables. Frowning, I put all my thought into shifting the water.

Seconds later, the mist hovering above the water began to swirl. Then the water beneath it bubbled. I smiled. I was doing it. A moment later, my smile faded, and my heart leapt into my throat when I realized I wasn't the one manipulating the river.

An enormous dark head rose from the water. Actually, it wasn't just one head, but three. Cerberus was as fearsome as I'd read in the books. Large eyes as red as blood and glowing like fire fixated on me. Three sets of jaws opened, razor sharp teeth as long as my forearm dripped with saliva, and thunderous growls emanated from within.

"Oh shit. Nice doggy."

The growls intensified, and the sound bounced off the rock. One stalactite broke from the ceiling and crashed down to the ground.

I whipped around and sprinted back the way I came.

I heard its giant paws scraping against the rock as it emerged from the river and into the cave. I kept running, as fast as I could, although I knew there was no way I could outrun it. Its one stride probably equaled ten of mine.

While I ran, fireballs formed in my hands. Without looking, I flung them over my shoulders, hoping to get lucky. I didn't. I formed some more and tossed them. Then I switched gears and tried to create lightning between my fingers. At first I only got a few sparks, but then I got a decent sized bolt. I stopped, turned, and hurled it at one of the stalactites hanging from above. My bolt hit one, it broke off, and fell, hitting Cerberus in its middle head. It yelped once, but it didn't stop.

"Shit." I spun and started running again.

Eventually, I came out of the cave and into a familiar looking hall. The ceilings were high, but I hoped it would be too short for the dog. I risked a quick glance over my shoulder. Nope. It was still coming; it just lowered its heads.

I searched for thick shadows along the wall, but every time I stepped into one, the firelight from the walls flared and vanquished the shadow. I wasn't going to find a way out. I was trapped. And that realization really smacked me down when I ran into the closed double doors leading to Hades Hall.

I tried the handles, but the doors were locked. I banged on them. "Let me in. Please!"

I felt Cerberus looming over me, and I slowly turned around to face it.

I craned my neck to look up into its three snarling

faces. Their black lips pulled back, and they bared their teeth.

I couldn't believe this was how I was going to die. I thought for sure it was going to be in battle after doing something daring and heroic.

"All right, doggo, you got me. Do your worst."

I ignited my hands with fire, splaying them out to the side. If I was going down, I wasn't going to go without a fight.

Cerberus lowered its middle head toward me, hot breath bathing my face. My nose wrinkled at the smell.

I lifted my hands, intending to inflict some damage, when its tongue came out and slobbered all over my face. Then it pulled back and tilted its middle head inquisitively. The other two heads did the same.

I stared at it, stunned I was still alive. "Um, why aren't you eating me?"

All three heads made a whining noise, and then it sat its big butt down onto the floor. The action vibrated the floor a little.

Closing my hands, I extinguished the flames. Then after taking a shaky breath, I reached up toward its middle head. I didn't know what to expect, but it definitely wasn't the nuzzle of its wet, rubbery nose against the palm of my hand.

A bubble of laughter gushed out of me. "Holy crap. You're a nice pupper, aren't you?"

It seemed to like that because its tongue came out again and licked my face. Then I was attacked by three very enthusiastic doggy tongues drenching me in stinky saliva.

Giggling, I pushed at their heads. "Stop it. You're disgusting."

All three of them whined. Obviously, they could understand my words.

"Aww, you're not disgusting. You're good boys."

That made them happy. All three heads lifted their lips and gave me doggy smiles, their tongues hanging out.

"I wish I had three huge treats to give you."

They kept smiling and panting.

"I bet I could find you something, if you took me across the river and back to the academy."

They stopped panting. Then each head shook back and forth.

Well, I had to try at least.

"Okay, can you take me back to my room at least?"

All three heads nodded up and down, their ears flapping. Smiling, I shook my head. Then the middle head lowered until its muzzle rested on the floor. It was an offer of a ride.

Keeping the other two heads in my sights, just in case, I climbed onto the middle head. When it came up, I buried my hands into its ruff and held on. Lifting a paw, Cerberus literally knocked on the door. It swung open.

I sighed, angry. "You're kidding me."

Cerberus carried me through the door and to my

room. Hades casually leaned up against the wall. He smiled when we approached.

"Ah, thank you for retrieving Melany."

One of the heads lowered, and Hades scratched it behind the ears.

The middle head dipped and I jumped down.

Then Hades ruffled the fur on all three heads, as they nuzzled their faces into him. "Good boys. Charon has your supper ready for you."

Cerberus turned and padded back down the hall. It passed through the door, and the door closed and locked behind it.

"Did you have a nice outing?" His look of amusement set my teeth on edge.

Before Hades could lecture me, I marched into my room. "Good night." I shut the door and then leaned up against it.

There was obviously no way out for me. I was stuck here for however long Hades wanted. I just wished I knew how long that would be. A week, a month, a year? The rest of my life? My stomach roiled at that thought.

CHAPTER EIGHT

MELANY

For the next couple of days, I trained with the Furies. At least I think it was only a couple of days. I couldn't be sure, as I had no sense of time down here. I didn't know when it was morning or night. I didn't see the sun or the moon. The only thing I had to guide me was the ringing of the bell to wake me up, and the moment when the Furies told me I was done training. Then I would drag my ass back to my room, eat something, shower or bath, and then sleep. I assumed I trained during the day and slept through the night, but I didn't really know.

Hades never invited me for dinner again. In fact I hadn't seen him since that night I tried to escape. I was disappointed, which surprised me to no end. I hated that it bothered me so much. It was a distraction.

And that distraction awarded me with a hard blow to the shoulder pad I wore by Allecto, who wielded a broadsword. Pain rumbled down my arm as I stumbled sideways and nearly lost my balance.

"You're lucky you're wearing protection, or your arm would be dangling from your body right now held on only by a few tendons and some strips of muscle."

The image of that made my stomach churn.

"Gross." Tisiphone laughed from her perch on top of the climbing wall as she watched me and Allecto spar with swords.

Allecto was always very vivid about the carnage she would have been able to inflict on me due to my stupid misjudgments and mistakes. And those lately had been plenty.

"I don't know where your mind is, but it needs to be here, focused. If this was a real battle, you would already be dead." Allecto shook her head.

I rolled my eyes. According to her, I'd been dead ten times in the past two hours. I figured I looked pretty good for a zombie.

She raised her sword. "Let's go again."

I lifted my sword; my back ached from the movement. I'd been training with my wings out and folded against my back. It was surprising how much extra weight they put on me. But I felt stronger than I did the day before, so it was working.

I stood at an angle with my left foot in front, both hands on the hilt, elbows close to the body, just as I was taught. Allecto swung from her left. I took a step back to avoid her attack. Her sword brushed by me, the tip mere inches from my chest, and then I shuffled to my right, and brought my sword around to strike her in the flank. But she was quick and had her sword back over to defend. The clash of our steel blades echoed through the room.

Back and forth we went, striking and defending, striking and defending, until sweat dripped off my forehead and soaked the back of my shirt. By the time she called it quits, my arms shook with the strain of holding up and swinging around three pounds of forged steel.

I wondered if Hephaistos made all the weapons here. I assumed so, which then made me think about my friends back at the academy. I wondered what kind of training they were doing. I wondered if Georgina had already learned how to move the very Earth itself. I smiled, thinking if she hadn't, she would eventually.

Jasmine probably led cadets in weapons training. She had a knack for the spear. I'd seen her do the coolest spins with it. I imagined her being a giant pain in Ares's ass. At least I hoped she was.

And Lucian…

I sighed, thinking about him. I missed him. I missed the way his smile made my insides quiver, and I missed how his lips made mine tingle from the briefest touch. I missed sparring with him in Heracles's class and the stolen moments we took flying around the grounds together, finding secret places just for us.

"Think fast!" The bottled water Tisiphone threw at me nearly beaned me in the head. It clipped my shoulder and landed on the floor.

"What the hell?" I picked it up and unscrewed the cap.

The plastic bottles of water here always threw me off, considering it was the only modern item I'd seen in a long while. Despite Hades's slick purple and blue suits, the hall had a very medieval type vibe. Well, that and the iPod Tisiphone had strapped to her forearm. She'd sometimes fly around with earbuds in and her music playing. I discovered her favorite music was from the 80s. She thought Billy Idol was the hottest man on the planet.

I took a swig of water.

"What were you thinking about?" Tisiphone came and plunked herself down beside me on the floor. "You had that dreamy look reserved only for guys."

"My friends. I was just wondering what kind of training they are doing."

"I guarantee you they aren't training like this."

"You're going to be ten times the warrior." Megaera slid into the conversation after touching down from hovering nearby. I hadn't even noticed her flying around. "Everyone's going to be jealous of your skills."

I frowned. "I don't think so. They aren't like that."

Megaera pulled a face. "Everyone is like that. Believe me."

"Well, if I could see them and train with them, then maybe I could put that to the test. But no, I'm stuck here like a freaking prisoner and Hades is my jailer." I drank the rest of the water, put on the cap, and then tossed the empty over my shoulder.

"Jailer is such a common term. I prefer guardian or overseer."

I bolted to my feet and whipped around to see Hades standing there, the empty water bottle clutched in his hand. He looked sleek and handsome in a tight black shirt and form fitting pants, similar to the training gear I wore. The shirt emphasized an extremely athletic chest and arms.

"How's the training going?" He glanced at Allecto as she joined us.

"Satisfactory. She has some skills but still lots to learn."

He then looked at me. "How do you think you are doing?"

I licked my lips, unsure of what to say. I felt like this was some sort of test, and if I said the wrong thing, I was going to be punished in some way. But I figured what was the worst that could happen that hadn't already happened. I was locked away in a gilded prison like Rapunzel or some shit.

"Okay, but I'd do better if I could train with my peers. If I'm going to be a soldier in the Gods Army, wouldn't it make sense that I learn how to fight with *that* army?"

His smile bloomed on his face, changing his demeanor completely. It was disarming when he did that.

"I'll make you a deal. If you beat me in a contest of skill, I'll let you go to the academy to train with your... friends."

My heart dropped into my stomach. What the hell could I ever beat Hades at? It was all just to humor me.

"What skill?"

"You choose."

I thought about all the things I'd learned so far. I was good with a sword and spear and the bow, but I suspected he'd be better as he had thousands of years of extra training. Hand to hand combat was out; he was stronger than I was, and he was a God for Pete's sake. I was a great flyer, but again he was Hades; he was born with wings I suspected. There was no way I could out do him even on my best day.

Then I thought of something, and I had to fight from grinning.

"Can I choose absolutely anything?"

He pulled a suspicious face but shrugged. "Sure."

Half an hour later, Hades and I stood at the far end of the training arena.

"This is ridiculous." He shook his head.

"Hey, you said anything."

"But this is not a skill."

"Sure it is." I hefted up the enormous, meaty leg bone. I didn't even want to consider what kind of animal it came from. All I cared about was whether it helped me win this contest. "At the academy, Artemis trained us in how to handle various beasts. It is definitely a skill."

I looked down the length of the arena and prayed I hadn't overestimated my ability to entice a five hundred pound, twenty foot, three-headed puppy. Cerberus sat on the floor waiting for Tisiphone and Megaera to let go of his leash. His tail thumped so hard it vibrated the entire floor.

After that night I had tried to escape and met Hades's guard dog, I'd snuck out a few times and brought him treats. I was hoping that had endeared him to me. I was relying on an assumption that Hades didn't show the dog a lot of affection, whereas I had. I'd given him many head scratches and belly rubs.

Hades picked up another meaty bone, gave me a jeering look, and then moved farther down the room, away from me, so there could be a clear winner of Cerberus's affections.

Once we were both in position, Tisiphone and Megaera released their hold on the leash.

"C'mere boys," I said, as I tried to lift the bone up into the air. It was damn heavy.

Hades didn't have that problem, and he waved the bone around. "A nice big treat for you. Yummy."

I nearly burst into laughter at Hades saying the

word yummy. He looked comical as well, waving the big bone around like a flag. Cerberus sniffed the air and then padded toward his master.

"Cerberus. Come here. Come to Melany." I hefted the big bone over my head like I was deadlifting a hundred pound barbell.

He stopped for a moment, turned his heads toward me, sniffed the air, and whined.

"Boy! Come here right now!" Hades's voice was stern, echoing through the studio.

Cerberus ducked his heads down.

"I'll give you lots and lots of belly rubs!" I wriggled the bone. "And kisses!" I added.

That was the winner.

Cerberus bounded over to me, tongues hanging out. I set down the bone for him, but he wasn't ready to eat yet. I had to make good on my promises.

"Good boy." I scratched all three heads behind the ears, moved my hands down, and rubbed his big belly. He flopped over onto his back. I laughed as I ruffled his fur with my hands.

Hades walked over and shook his head, but I caught his smile. "Traitor." There was no malice in his tone.

He dropped the bone down next to the other.

Cerberus rolled onto his feet, and then two of the heads chomped down on the bones.

I couldn't wipe the smile from my face as I watched him devour the treat.

Hades sighed. "I suppose you won, although I feel like you cheated."

"Regardless, I won the bet. And you better keep your word."

He nodded. "You can go in a sennight." He moved toward the door.

"What the hell is a sennight?"

But he didn't answer me; he just left.

I walked over to Tisiphone and Megaera, who had been watching it all gleefully.

"What is a sennight? It better be like his version of tomorrow."

Tisiphone patted me on the shoulder. "It's a week.

I gaped at her. "A week? That's too long."

"Just be happy you're going at all." She extended her wings and flapped them. "C'mon, you still got training to do."

I should've been happy that I'd gotten the better of Hades, but in fact it was a moot point. I'd done nothing but showed myself to be a fool. To think I could get the upper hand on him. That was never going to happen no matter what I did. I hated that he had all this power over me. But he did, and I supposed I was just going to have to learn to live with it. Even if it made every atom of my being pulse with defiance.

CHAPTER NINE

LUCIAN

The lake came into view as we flew up as high as we could while still being able to breathe. I led one of the six-member squads in the exercise with my wing mates Jasmine and Diego on my left and right, respectively. Like fighter jets, we were learning to fly in formation. Our goal, set by Hermes, was to reach around five hundred feet in the air, maintain it, and then descend to the lake's shore.

I loved flying. It was one of my favorite things to do at the academy. Deep down, I kind of wished I'd been called to Hermes's clan, so I could be in the air all the time. But I knew my love of it and my skill, along with my affinity to lightning, had gotten me into Zeus's clan, which was a good place to be. It was a clan of leaders.

I pushed a little more until I thought we had reached our goal, and then checked over my shoulder at my team to make sure everyone was in proper formation. Mia, who flew behind Diego, struggled a little, but after a few moments she was able to get in line with Ren and Georgina. We flew like that for a few minutes.

Pride swelled inside me. We'd been working well together for the past two weeks. I was glad I had my friends in my squad. I didn't know what I would've done if Hermes had put me in Revana's squad. Although I'd have gone along with it, I imagined. I wasn't sure if I was I cut out to be a rebel.

That made me think of Melany. She would've kicked, punched, and screamed her way out of that situation. Or she would've pushed herself to the front position of that squad and forced Revana out. I smiled, thinking about her, but it faded when I thought about how long it had been since she'd disappeared.

None of us knew if we'd ever see her again. Every time I asked anyone, like Zeus or Demeter or Hephaistos, anyone who would listen for a moment, I got the same answer: "I'm sure she's fine and will return soon."

Once we reached our target height, I gestured to the group to start our descent to the lake. With me in the lead, we dove down. I reveled in the way my body felt zipping through the air. Flying was so freeing.

As we swooped over the tall trees surrounding the lake, it reminded me of all the times Melany and I had escaped the academy and gone on several secret flights. One time we even followed Dionysus into these woods and crashed one of his strange but fun parties with a bunch of wood nymphs and a satyr or two.

Nearing the lake's shore, I heard the sounds of more flapping coming from behind my squad. I looked over to see Revana and her crew coming in fast to the same spot we'd planned on landing. Before I could react, Revana collided with Georgina and knocked her from the sky. Georgina crashed in a heap on the rocky shore of the lake.

The rest of us landed and immediately rushed to Georgina's aid. She was getting up but on shaky legs. Revana and her group landed a few feet away. Jasmine was up in Revana's face before I could do anything about it.

"You did that on purpose." Jasmine's hands clenched into fists.

Revana smirked. "Not likely. Your girl there just doesn't know how to fly. She should stick to what she knows best… gardening."

That had the others in her group snickering.

Now that Isobel had been punted from the academy, Revana had two other nasty little minions, Peyton and Klara, to laugh at her pettiness. I didn't know how I'd managed to stay friendly with her for so long. Before we came to the academy, she was snide and snobbish, but over the past few months, she'd just gotten petty and mean, really mean.

The ground beneath our feet started to rumble. A couple of vines burst through the rocks and wound their way toward Revana. One got very close to strangling her around the neck.

I stepped in. "Can we just put all this crap aside and work together? That's what we're supposed to be doing. We are not each other's enemies."

Revana smirked as the vines slunk back into the ground. I glanced over at Georgina, and she lowered her hands.

"Ever the peacekeeper." Revana took a few steps toward me, a finger twirling in her hair. "You know, Lucian, now that the trash is gone, there's no reason for you to stay on the lower-class side of the academy."

"You bitch." Jasmine went to charge at her, but I grabbed her before she could.

"Revana, every time you open your mouth you prove just how classless you are. You may have been born to money, but it certainly didn't buy you any common decency."

Jasmine laughed. "Oh snap."

"Whatever. You'll change your mind once I'm made overall squad leader. I mean, honestly, you're not really much without your pet. However much I hated her, I can't deny she was a fierce fighter. It's too bad she's not ever coming back. From what I hear, she's happy being shacked up with a God. I mean Hades is pretty easy on the eyes." Revana turned and walked away, her group following her.

I watched her go, her words drilling into me hard.

"Don't listen to her," Jasmine said.

"Mel would come back if she could," Georgina added.

"It's been over a month. What if she's right and—"

"She's full of shit, Lucian." Jasmine picked up a rock from the shore and skipped it across the water. "Mel will be back."

"I can't wait for that. Let's break her out."

Everyone gaped at me. "What do you mean, break her out?" Ren asked.

"Let's go to Hades Hall, break in, and bring Mel back here."

"There could be consequences," he said.

"I don't care."

"Do you even know where Hades Hall is?" Georgina asked.

"No, but I'm sure we can find someone who does."

The more I thought about it, the more determined I was. I couldn't stand that Melany had been gone so long. I knew she was probably sitting there wondering why we hadn't come to get her yet. I didn't want to disappoint her any longer.

"Tonight, we're going to rescue Mel and bring her home."

We agreed to meet just outside at the entrance to the maze at midnight. It wouldn't be easy for any of us to sneak out of our clan areas. Zeus Hall was in the highest tower of the academy, and the staircases were patrolled by various academy monitors. I called them guards, but I'd been assured that no one was stopping us from roaming the academy halls freely. Of course that was bullshit, as I'd been stopped before.

So instead of taking the stairs, I opened a window in my dorm room, and jumped out, my wings making an appearance before I plummeted to my death. I flew around the monstrous stone building that was the academy and landed in the gardens near the maze.

Jasmine, Georgina, and Ren were already there waiting. I'd told Diego and Mia not to come, as a smaller group would be less noticeable. Jasmine wasn't happy with me about that, as she didn't get a lot of time to spend with Mia.

"Okay, we're here. Now what?" Jasmine shrugged.

"Now, we wait."

"For what?" she asked.

A dark form stepped out of the maze. "For me, I imagine."

Dionysus lumbered into a pool of moonlight. He looked a bit unsteady; he was constantly leaning to his right.

Jasmine scowled. "Oh, you're joking, right?"

"Are you drunk?" I asked.

He shrugged. "That's a matter of perspective."

I shook my head, too anxious to find Melany to care. "You told me you could guide us to Hades Hall, so where do we go?"

"You need to find Hecate. She knows the way."

"Who the hell is Hecate?" Jasmine asked.

"She's the Goddess of witchcraft." Georgina's voice was so low she was almost whispering.

"Yes, but her disciples are the Lampades, who are nymphs of the underworld. Hades Hall is in the underworld," Dionysus said.

"Where do we find Hecate?" I asked.

"In the woods. Near the lake's shore, look for the largest oak tree. You'll find Hecate nearby." He took out a flask from his jacket pocket and took a swig. "Now, if you'll excuse me, I have some serious drinking to do."

He gave me a curt nod, and then he stumbled away toward the back entrance of the academy, muttering to himself.

"Okay, let's go." I unfurled my wings to get ready to fly.

Georgina shivered. "Hecate is not someone we want to mess with."

"I'll deal with evil incarnate if it means getting to Melany." I flapped my wings, rising into the air. If the others didn't want to come, I was fine with that. But after a few seconds, Jasmine and Ren joined me. Then Georgina finally unfurled her wings and flew up next to us.

When we reached the lake, we touched down on the shore, not far from where we'd been earlier in the day during training. Jasmine created a small ball of fire in her hand for light, and then we walked along the edge of the woods looking for the biggest oak tree.

It didn't take us long to find it. It wasn't that it was tall, as much as it was wide. The trunk had to have been more than thirty feet in circumference, and its branches were so big and heavy that a few of them touched the ground, spreading out along the forest floor. From one angle, it looked like a giant spider with eight sprawling legs.

"Now what?" Jasmine asked.

Frowning, I walked around the tree, searching for something. I wasn't sure what, but there was something odd about the surface on one side of the trunk. There was a large crack down the bark, all the way to the ground. It didn't look natural.

I touched the trunk; it still felt like bark, but I couldn't help but think there was something different about it. I knocked my hand against it. There was a hollow echoing that resounded around me.

A cracking noise came from the tree. I took a step back as a portion of the trunk moved, swinging toward me. It was a door. Before I could remark on it, a tall, willowy woman with black hair hanging to her waist stepped out. She had a long wooden walking stick in her hand.

"Who knocks upon Hecate's door?" Her voice was lilting, musical, and very pleasant.

"Um, I do."

When she turned to look at me, the light from Jasmine's fireball fell upon her face. She was beautiful, with pale, flawless skin and ruby red lips.

"What is your name?"

"Lucian."

Her gaze then turned to the others. "What is it you want Lucian and companions?"

"We want to go to Hades Hall."

She frowned. "Why?"

"To save our friend," I said.

Her eyes narrowed. Then another voice spoke; it was gravely, old sounding. "A girl. He wants to save his girl."

I didn't know where the voice came from, but it was close by. Behind her, maybe, from inside the tree?

"Who told you to come?"

"Dionysus. He said you'd help us."

"Liar. The boy lies!" The other voice came again.

Then Hecate started to shake and convulse.

"Are you okay?" For a brief second, I thought about reaching out to her.

Stunned, I watched as her head turned ninety degrees. The sound of her bones cracking and twisting made my stomach roil.

Jasmine, Georgina, and Ren all jumped back, as a different face glared at me.

This one was old and haggard with rheumy eyes, a crooked nose, and liver spots all over her sallow cheeks. And when she spoke, she revealed rotten brown teeth.

"You lie, boy. Dionysus would never send you here."

"He did." Jasmine stepped forward. "He said you'd know the way to the underworld, to Hades Hall. How else do you think we found you?"

"Shut up, girl. We are not talking to you." She lifted the walking stick and pointed it menacingly at Jasmine.

Hecate's body began to shake again, like she was having a seizure, and then her head twisted back. "I'm sorry about that." She smiled at me, and I was enchanted by her again. "For the path to Hades, you must pay a price."

"What price?" I asked, although I was leery about what she'd demand from us.

"Your blood."

Ren stepped forward and grabbed my arm to pull me away. "You can forget that, lady."

But I didn't move. "How much?"

She smiled again, and it was sweet and alluring, and I suddenly wanted to fall at her feet. "Not much, just an ounce, not more. I need the blood of a champion for my spells." She reached out a long, slim hand and caressed my face. "You look like a champion."

"Deal."

"This is stupid, Lucian." Jasmine shook her head. "You're stupid for agreeing to this."

"I'll do whatever it takes to find Melany. She'd do it for me."

For a moment, I thought Jasmine was going to say, "No she wouldn't," but she sighed and didn't say anything else.

"So, how do you take it? A knife?" I raised my arm toward Hecate.

She gently held my arm in both her hands. "You will need to be very still for this."

Her head twitched and spasmed again, and then it turned, but the opposite way from before. I didn't know what I was looking at, but it wasn't a face. It was some horrifying amalgamation of human and animal. Before I could react, its maw opened, revealing rows of long, pointy teeth, some of them like needles, then the jaws snapped shut on my arm and I screamed.

The pain was searing, burning through my skin and flesh. I tried to pummel her head with my other hand, but it was to no avail. She was strong, gripping my arm tight in her claw-like hands. I felt my blood being sucked from my veins.

Ren, Jasmine, and Georgina all rushed toward Hecate, but she released my arm, took a step back, and I heard the squishy noise of her teeth coming out of my flesh. She raised her hands toward my friends, freezing them in place. They could no longer move. Only their eyes were left mobile to blink.

The creature snarled and growled, then it shook and spasmed, and Hecate's original pretty face came back into view. She reached into the clothes she wore, pulling out a small glass bottle. She put it to her lips and spit out my blood into the container. My stomach churned, and I nearly retched up the meager meal I'd had hours ago. When she was done regurgitating my blood, she wiped her mouth with her hand, streaks of red glaring against her pale skin, and slid the bottle back into a pocket in her robe.

"Thank you, Lucian." She bowed her head and then waved her hand in the air, releasing my friends from their frozen state.

I looked down at my arm, amazed as the holes she'd bitten into my skin knitted back together. There was no longer sharp pain, but a deep throb.

"What the hell was that?" Jasmine growled.

Hecate stepped aside from the tree and waved her hand toward the entrance. "Hades Hall is down the stairs and through the tunnel."

I frowned. What stairs?

"Come." She gestured for us to step into the tree.

Ren grabbed my shoulder. "This doesn't feel right."

I shook him off; I was determined to find Melany at any cost. I stepped through the door in the tree, uncaring if the others followed me. After some hesitation, they finally did.

Inside the tree defied the laws of physics. It was as spacious as my dorm room with a small bed and kitchen and table and chair. Curved along one wall were shelves crammed full with glass bottles and herbs and plants.

Hecate gestured to the floor in the corner. I stepped up to it and peered down into a hole. There were crudely built stairs in the wood and dirt spiraling down into darkness.

"The stairs will take you to a tunnel. There you will be greeted by Orphne, who will guide you the rest of the way."

"Thank you." I started down into the hole, cautious that I didn't slip on the stairs, as they weren't very sturdy. Jasmine followed me in, another ball of fire in her hand to light our way. Georgina came next, then Ren last.

I didn't know how far we descended, but I'd counted the steps in my mind. Eighty-five steps down into the Earth. When we reached the bottom it was, as Hecate had said, into a dirt tunnel. I was thankful it wasn't as narrow as I thought it was going to be, as the air down here was stale and thick, not pleasant to breathe in.

I looked at the others. "Anyone claustrophobic?"

They shook their heads.

"No, but I am thirsty," Georgina said. "And none of us thought to bring a canteen."

"Hold on." Ren reached into the air, bringing his hand down. Cupped inside his hand was a small pool of water. He brought it to Georgina's mouth. It was a bit awkward, but she managed to drink the water he'd captured. "Anyone else?"

I shook my head, as did Jasmine. Then I peered into the pitch black tunnel. "Looks like we're on our own." Before we could enter, I spied a yellow glow in the darkness, and it grew closer by the second.

Eventually, the glow manifested itself as a small, bald woman, warm yellow light shining through her translucent skin.

"Are you Orphne?"

She nodded and gestured for us to follow her into the tunnel.

I asked her a bunch of questions about Hades and his hall as we trudged through the tunnel, but she didn't answer. She either couldn't talk or wouldn't. Maybe Ren and Jasmine's reservations were warranted, and we were walking into some kind of trap. I wasn't sure I really cared; all I wanted was to see Melany. I needed to know she was okay.

After I didn't know how long—time seemed to be distorted down here, I could feel it move differently—Orphne led us out of the tunnel, which opened up into a huge underground cavern and into a marsh. Beyond that I could hear the rush of raging water.

"Where do we go?"

She pointed toward the sound of water, and then she returned to the tunnel, which appeared to be dug out of the core of the Earth.

Out of nowhere, a sense of dread washed over me.

Maybe it was just this place and getting nearer to Hades Hall and Hades himself. I didn't want to consider that we were walking into something ominous.

We crossed the marsh with ease. Moonlight illumined the way, or at least I thought it was moonlight, although when I looked up at the cavern ceiling, I didn't see any breaks in the rock. Then we stood on the shore of a dark raging river that I identified as the river Styx—the barrier between this world and the underworld. Between us and Melany.

"How do we cross it?" Jasmine asked, as she stood beside me and looked out over the turbulent water. "Can we swim it?"

I shook my head. "Too wild. We'd get swept downstream and end up Gods know where." I looked over at Ren. "What do you think? Could you create a path through it?"

"I can try." Ren took a few steps forward, so the toes of his boots touched the water's edge. Crouching, he thrust his hands into the river.

I watched him as he clamped his eyes shut, his brow furrowing, deeper and deeper, until his eyes snapped open again, and he glared out over the water. I didn't know what I expected, the bubbling of the river maybe, the parting of the water, but I didn't expect what we got—nothing.

Ren stood, shaking his head. "It won't respond to me."

I kicked at the rocks on the shore. "Damn it." I refused to be stopped. I had to get to Melany.

I thought about charging up my hands, but lightning wasn't going to do anything for us, except maybe get us all electrocuted. Electricity and water were a deadly mixture.

I glanced at Georgina. "Can you make us a bridge of some sort?"

She bent down and touched the pebbles lining the river's shore. She dug her fingers past them and into the ground. She kept digging, and her brow furrowed like Ren's had. Eventually, she stood. "I can't either. The ground won't talk to me."

I unfurled my wings out from my back and flapped them once. "We'll fly over." I flapped again, but the air felt different here. Thick and constricting. I couldn't get off the ground. It was like trying to fly through viscous liquid. I guessed we weren't flying anywhere. I folded my wings back.

"Shit!" I pounded my fists against my legs. How could we have come this far, only to be stopped from going any farther? It wasn't fair. "There has to be a way across."

Jasmine gripped my arm, gesturing with her head. "Look."

Across the river, I could see the mouth of a large cave, and something emerged from it. It was a large, black creature with three sets of glowing red eyes.

"It's Cerberus," Georgina said. "Hades's guard dog."

As the creature got closer, I could see someone rode on top of it. The three-headed dog stopped at the river's edge, and the person slid down onto the ground. It was Melany. I'd recognize that blue hair anywhere.

My heart jumped into my throat at the sight of her.

Smiling, she waved. "Hey." Her voice carried across the water, and it was like soothing music to my ears.

I waved back. "Blue, we're here to rescue you!"

"I don't need rescuing, Lucian."

Confused, I darted a quick glance at Jasmine. She was frowning just as hard as I was. "Mel, you've been gone for a long time. You should come back with us."

"I'm exactly where I need to be, Jas. I'm learning so much."

"Blue…?"

"I'm okay. I promise. Don't worry about me."

I didn't understand. Surely, she wanted to come back to the academy. To be with her friends, to be with me.

"I want to be here. I want to train with Hades. He's not who you think he is. Zeus and Poseidon lie about him."

I glanced at the others, wondering if they were buying this. The looks on their faces matched mine— confusion, sorrow.

"Go back to the academy. Don't come for me again," Melany said.

"Blue." I took a few steps forward, the river gushing over my boots. I could feel it pulling at me, trying to take me down. But I wouldn't let it. "I... I love you. Please come back with us."

I wasn't sure what I expected in return. A declaration of her love maybe, but all I got was a smile and another wave. Then she climbed back onto Cerberus and the big creature turned and lumbered back into the cave.

I felt Ren's hand on my shoulder. "Come on, let's go back."

I didn't say anything, just stared out over the river at Cerberus's retreating back.

Jasmine put her hand on my arm and tugged me out of the water. "She's made her choice, Lucian. I don't understand it, but she probably has a reason for it."

I stepped away from the river and turned around, starting across the marsh. The others fell in step with me. No one spoke, which I was grateful for. I had no words for this crushing feeling inside. I didn't think I could explain it to anyone so I didn't try.

Head down, I concentrated on my steps and not on the despair rolling over me.

CHAPTER TEN

MELANY

I bolted straight up in bed, sweat covering my body and my heart hammering in my chest. I took in a few gasping breaths as the remnants of my nightmare still lingered in my mind. I scrubbed at my face with my hands, trying to brush the horrifying images away.

I'd dreamt about Lucian, Jasmine, Georgina, and Ren. They'd stood on the opposite shore of the Styx River, shouting my name. Then the dark water started to bubble and boil. From the swirling river, a large black creature emerged. It had been Cerberus. Growling and gnashing his teeth, he'd leaned down and tore at my friends. Blood and body parts had spewed into the air. I'd seen Lucian's throat torn open. Their collective screams still echoed in my ears and I shuddered violently.

The worst part of the nightmare was I'd ridden on top of Cerberus, laughing at it all. My stomach sloshed, and I thought I might get sick.

I tossed aside the blanket, rolling out of bed. When I stood, my legs wobbled a little, but I forced myself to walk into the bathroom. At the sink, I filled the basin with ice cold water then dunked my face into it. I stayed submersed until my skin stung from the biting cold, and I could no longer hold my breath.

I refused to stay a prisoner any longer. I wanted to see my friends.

After I dried my face, I threw on a black robe over my pajamas and marched out of my room and down the corridor. I was going to find Hades and demand to be allowed to return to the academy. The thing was I had no idea which door led to his room.

I checked the library first but he wasn't there. Then I looked in the dining room, also empty. Just in case, I checked the training studio. It was also empty, or at least I think it was. I heard some rustling up near the ceiling, so it was highly possible the Furies were perched up on a ledge. Did they sleep there? Weird.

That left two rooms to check.

I tried the door right across from my bedroom. It was locked. I jiggled the handle over and over, hoping if he was in there, he'd get annoyed enough to come open the door. But that didn't work and it stayed locked. I marched across the corridor to the other closed door. I tried it and it, too, was locked.

"Damn it." But I refused to give up.

If using the shadows to get past the main doors worked, I could do it here. Looking for a deep shadow near the door, I found one, and quickly stepped into it before I lost my nerve. I reached out with my hands and gathered more of the darkness around me, until I was completely shrouded in the gloom and the corridor faded.

I could feel the change in the air, the buoyancy of it, like floating in salt water. Taking in a breath, I moved through the darkness trusting I was going the right way. After a few steps, I searched the shadows for a pinpoint of light. I found it, moved toward it, and then stepped out into another room.

It was a bedroom suite similar to mine, but twice the size. Of course Hades would have a bedroom the size of an entire floor in a castle. The room was dimly lit by a low fire crackling in the hearth. It cast a warm orange glow over all the furniture and bookshelves and the canopied bed on the far side.

I marched over to it. The dark curtains were drawn around the bed, so I didn't know for sure if he was there, but I thought it was safe to make the assumption. I felt odd confronting him in his bedroom. I felt a bit uncomfortable with the fact that he could be sleeping naked or even have a companion under the sheets with him.

But it still didn't stop me from gripping one of the drapes and yanking it aside.

He was there, lying on the bed, fully clothed thank the Gods, eyes closed, his hands resting on top of his chest. He looked dead. Like Dracula asleep in his coffin. It was a bit unsettling looking down at him.

Then his eyes blinked open and I jumped back.

"If you had a bad dream, you can't sleep with me. It would be inappropriate." He sat up and swung his legs over the side of the bed.

"That's not why I'm here."

"Then why are you here? In my bedroom at this late hour?" One eyebrow rose with amused curiosity.

Something pricked at my mind, and I frowned at him. "How did you know I had a bad dream?"

"Lucky guess." He got to his feet and scratched at the stubble on his chin. "Is that why you're here then?"

"I demand to return to the academy."

He brushed past me and walked over to the wooden stand near the fireplace. He picked up a glass decanter of what I assumed was water and poured some in a glass. Lifting the decanter, he glanced at me. "Do you want some water?"

"No." Then remembering myself, I added, "Thank you."

He drank the water and then turned to me. "You woke me up to demand to return to the academy?"

"Yes."

"Do you wish to go now in the middle of the night while everyone is sleeping?"

"No. But I didn't want to wait until you disappeared somewhere like you do sometimes when I'm training. I thought it was best to catch you by surprise, so I could tell you what I wanted."

He made a face. "Okay, you've told me. Now, can I go back to bed?" He yawned and stretched.

I took a couple steps toward him. We were a mere foot apart. I could smell the spiced cologne he always wore. It was light and subtle and pleasant. He grinned as if he knew what I was thinking. The light from the fire danced in his dark eyes and I shivered.

I cleared my suddenly clogged throat. "I want your word that you'll let me return to the academy tomorrow."

His gaze travelled my face, spent too much time lingering on my mouth for my liking, then came back to my eyes, gazing deep inside. "You can return to train. They are doing a mock war game tomorrow, and then you must come back here."

"Why can't I stay up top for a few days? I could stay in——"

"No. It's out of the question. It's not how it works, Melany." He moved to the fire, picked the poker, and stoked the flames. "Every cadet must stay in their assigned clan."

"Why? What's going to happen if we don't? Is the world going to fall apart?" I knew I was pushing him, but I was tired of the rules. I hated rules.

"It's how it's done. In a past age, it wasn't like that, but now under Zeus's lightning fist…" He poked the fire again. "If we want to stay, we have to play."

"What do you mean a past age? How old is the academy? I thought it was just over a hundred years old."

"Too many questions. You're giving me a headache." He put the poker away and turned to look at me. "You can have your day at the academy with your friends. Be happy with that." His eyes flashed again, but it wasn't from the fire in the hearth.

He frightened me. I wasn't going to lie to myself and say he didn't. But I wasn't going to let him continually push me around, so I didn't back up when he moved toward me, knowing he wanted me to. I stood my ground.

"Don't push me, Melany. I've given you a lot of leeway since your arrival. Don't make me put on the restraints."

"Fine. You can go back to sleep now." I turned and marched toward the door.

"Good night, Melany. Have sweet dreams."

I froze in the doorway, swiveling to look at him. He gave me a wink, and my blood ran cold.

I continued out of his room, hurrying to mine. I climbed into bed and pulled the blankets up to my chin. Although I was still tired, I didn't think I could go back to sleep. Hades had sent me that dream; I was sure of it. And now that I'd gotten in his face, I feared what he'd send me next.

CHAPTER ELEVEN

MELANY

*W*hen the wake-up bell rang, I was already awake, sitting up in bed and staring into the darkness, anxious to see my friends. I jumped out of bed, did all my washing, and then went into my closet to get dressed. It shouldn't have surprised me to see only one outfit hanging in my closet; all the rest of the clothes had vanished. Hades was obviously very concerned about appearances and didn't trust me to make the best decision about that.

I took the pieces off the hangers—black leather pants, black leather waist harness, dark purple shirt made with that same armored material as my training outfit, black cowl, and hooded cape. Included were heavy-duty, ankle-length black boots that had dark purple stitching. I put everything on and looked at myself in the mirror. I resembled a post-apocalyptic Robin Hood. I grinned. I was completely badass.

After I finished dressing, I made my way to the dining room for breakfast. Hades wasn't there, just the little serving robot to keep me company, but he left me a note next to my plate of eggs and sausage.

I will meet you in the library to show you how to get back to the academy. Hades
   P.S. Don't choke on your eggs from eating too fast.

I chuckled as I ate. Not only was he starting to know me pretty well, but I was starting to appreciate his sense of humor. And I wasn't sure how I felt about that.

"Too bad you can't talk, little dude," I said to the robot. "Then we could gossip about Hades."

The robot just blinked at me, but I imagined if it had a mouth, it would be smiling right now.

Despite Hades's warning, I did eat quickly but didn't choke on anything. I hurried across the corridor to the library eager to get to the academy. I spotted Hades near one of the bookcases, reading from one of the old books. When I stepped into the room, he turned and his face lit up.

The way he looked at me made me uncomfortable. Partly because he was my teacher, and partly because it made my insides tingle, and my belly performed a little flip flop. Which could become problematic.

He shut the book, slid it back onto the shelf, and then turned his attention on me. "I see I chose well. You look totally worthy of my clan."

"I thought I was worthy because of my skills."

He waved a hand at me. "Yes, of course, but it doesn't hurt to look fierce and capable of breaking a person in two now, does it?"

I couldn't stop the smile. "I suppose."

The surprised looks on my friends' faces was going to be so worth it. Especially Lucian. Oh, and I couldn't wait to see Revana's reaction. She was going to gag with jealousy.

"Right." He stepped close to me. "So, what I'm going to show you is secret. It's something only I know, and I'm going to trust you enough to share it."

I nodded, surprised by his comment, as I didn't think he trusted me at all. At least he hadn't acted like it over the past week, or couple of weeks? I wasn't even sure what day it was.

"Don't make me regret it."

"I won't."

"Disappearing into the shadows is the first step. I know you know how to walk through the shadows, short distances anyway, like from here to the river." He gave me a sidelong glance, obviously

knowing I had tried to escape the hall the other
night.

"What I'm going to show you is a way to transport
yourself from one place to another through the darkness. Like from here to the academy."

"Like a portal?"

He nodded. "It's a powerful ability, and one only
you will possess. None of your fellow cadets will ever
learn to do this."

"Can the other Gods do it?"

"Of course, but not through darkness. They use
other methods, which is why they can't just pop into my
hall."

"You mean Zeus can't just come here?"

"That's right. He has to cross the river and knock
on the door just like everyone else."

I smiled at that.

He caught my smile and returned it.

Then he reached into his pants pocket and pulled
out a black disc on a chain. He held it up toward me. It
was a silver necklace with a black wooden amulet on it.
"You must wear this at all times." He slipped it over my
head.

The amulet felt warm as it fell between my breasts.
My hand came up to touch it.

"It's made of ebony, from the giant tree in the hall.
It makes a connection to this place. It will help you
move around easily."

"It's beautiful."

He glanced at the amulet, then up at my face. "Yes, it is."

I frowned, confused if he was referring to the necklace or me.

"Now, stand here." He pointed to a spot right next to him. I obeyed. "Together, we will gather the darkness."

I felt uncomfortable doing this with Hades. I mean, he was the God of Darkness essentially. He could do all of this in his sleep and probably did. But I figured I could just suck it up and do it, or stay in this hall forever.

Concentrating on the shadows around us, I reached out and drew them closer. A prickling sensation rippled over my skin as the gloom shrouded us. I shivered at how quickly I could do it now. Maybe it was because I stood beside the master of the dark, or because I was starting to become like him. Either way, I smiled.

"Good," Hades said from beside me. I could see him there, but it was like looking at someone through a filter. A really hazy, dark filter. "Now, the next thing you need to do is to picture where you want to go."

"The dining hall," I blurted. "That's where I imagine everyone will be."

"Okay, so imagine it in your mind. Picture it clearly."

I shut my eyes and thought about the academy and the dining hall. I could see the dark wooden tables, polished to a shine. The immaculate white tiled floors.

The huge open doors that had intricate carvings in the wooden frames. I imagined Lucian and Jasmine and Georgina sitting at one of those tables together, eating pancakes with fruit and whipped cream, and the huge cup of coffee Lucian always had.

"I can see it."

"Good. Now, keep it in your mind and start walking. It'll feel weird at first, like you're marching through liquid honey. There will be some resistance, but push through it."

I felt the viscosity almost immediately. The air surrounding us was thick and cloying, almost sticky on my skin. It proved difficult to lift my leg and put it down to step forward. But I pushed through. Hades walked beside me with almost no effort at all.

He must've sensed my thoughts because he commented, "It'll stop being hard after you've done it a million times like I have."

Eventually, I was able to garner a decent walking pace, and then the air didn't feel so heavy.

"How will I know that I'm going in the right direction, and that I've arrived at my destination?"

"Practice."

I smirked. "That's not really helpful. What if I end up in some random closet in some random room I don't recognize or outside, a hundred miles away from where I want to be?"

"You can only go to places you've been before. There has to be some kind of connection." He pointed ahead of him. "Concentrate and you'll soon start to hear and see where you want to be."

I raised my head and looked forward. He was right. There was distant light up ahead, and I could hear the faint sounds of voices and laughter. That spurred me on, and I moved faster, determined to get out of the shadows and into the dining hall.

After a few more steps, the shadows started to wane, and it wasn't so difficult to move. I glanced at Hades, a smile creeping across my face.

"Remember, you have to return to the hall this evening. Hold the amulet in your hand, and it will take you there quickly." He stopped walking as I continued on.

Finally, I could see the light blossoming, and I aimed right for that growing circle. Then I stepped out onto the tiled floor of the dining hall. To those in the room, it would've looked like I just appeared out of nowhere.

The reactions I received didn't disappoint. And my ego just got stroked really hard.

"Holy shit!" I heard someone gasp.

I looked toward one of the voices and saw Diego's eyes bugging out. "Damn girl, you look like an assassin."

That made me grin.

"Blue!"

"Mel!"

Lucian, Jasmine, and Georgina rushed toward me.

They all tried to hug me at once, so it became an awkward group pile on, making me laugh.

Jasmine eyed me up and down. "What the hell are you wearing?" She poked her finger against my leather corset.

"Armor."

She frowned. "Really?"

I nodded. "Everything I'm wearing can deflect a blade."

"Wow." Jasmine touched my cape.

"I think you look amazing." Georgina smiled.

"You do look amazing." Lucian grinned.

"Gods, it's been so long since we've seen you." Georgina shook her head.

Lucian hugged me again. "I can't believe you're here."

I giggled. "You are all acting like I've been gone for months. It's only been a week or two."

I caught the look between Jasmine and Georgina. Lucian's brow furrowed.

I looked to each of them.

Lucian swallowed. "Mel, you've been in Hades Hall for two months."

"What?" I flinched. "You're messing with me."

"We're not." Jasmine shook her head. "It's been two months since the celebration when you disappeared. Two weeks since we saw you at the river."

My head started to swim and my knees buckled. Lucian caught me before I could collapse onto the floor. He helped me to the table nearby and sat me down, settling in beside me. His knee touched mine, and it helped me feel more grounded.

I shook my head, trying to rectify my experience to what they were telling me. "I swear it's been maybe two weeks for me. Time did feel different down there, as I didn't have a watch and had no access to the outside, but two months? I can't believe it." Then it hit me what Jasmine had said. Frowning, I looked up at her. "And what do you mean at the river? I haven't seen any of you since the big celebration."

They all shared a concerned look again. I hated that it made me feel like an outsider. They'd had two months together without me, making new memories that I'd never be privy to.

Lucian grabbed my hand. "I knew it wasn't you."

"Explain what's going on," I demanded.

Jasmine sighed. "About two weeks ago, we found a way down to the underworld. We planned on breaking you out of Hades Hall…"

Georgina picked up the story. "But when we got to the river Styx, we couldn't get across. None of our powers would work."

"Then across the river we saw Cerberus. And you were riding it, and you told us to go back and to forget about you. That you were happy where you were." Lucian squeezed my hand. "But I knew it wasn't you."

My stomach churned. I gripped the table, my fingers digging in until my knuckles turned white.

Anger surged through me. I couldn't believe Hades would do that to me. And here I was starting to like my training, starting to like him even. Why would he do that? Why was it so important to keep me away from my friends, away from the academy?

CHAPTER TWELVE

MELANY

"Was it Hades?" Lucian asked. The look in his eyes was a mixture of anger and sorrow. And it pained me to see it there. I knew I hadn't betrayed him, but I still felt responsible.

I nodded. "He really doesn't want me to be here. I had to jump through hoops just to get a day pass."

"That sonofabitch." Lucian clenched his hand into a fist. I saw a few white sparks flying off his fingers. "Why?"

"I don't know." But I sort of did, didn't I? It was becoming evident that maybe Hades looked at me as more than a student. I felt his gaze on me sometimes. It was a searching look, curiosity definitely, and something more maybe. The distressing thing was I liked it. But

I'd never say it out loud, not to anyone, especially not Lucian.

Jasmine gave me side-eye, as if she knew the answer and didn't approve.

Before we could discuss it further, a loud horn blast echoed through the halls of the academy, making everyone jump. Lucian stood.

"What was that?" I watched as cadets started to stream out of the dining hall.

"The call to battle." He grabbed my hand and pulled me up. "It's part of our training today. It's a mock battle, executed as if it was really happening." Together, we moved toward the exit.

"What's the goal?"

"To not get killed." Jasmine snorted.

"We're supposed to band together as a group and keep the enemy from reaching the academy."

"Who's the enemy?" As we walked, my gaze caught Revana glaring at me, her eye daggers were lethal.

Lucian shook his head. "Don't know. Could be anyone. Gods, demigods. We have to be prepared for anything."

All forty or so of us gathered just outside the main door to the academy. A makeshift armory had been set up on the grounds. Rows of weapons including swords, spears, axes, hammers, and bows and arrows leaned up against one wooden stand. All of them were blunted, so we didn't actually kill anyone. I imagined it would be similar to the mock battle we had for the twelfth trial, like a really big brutal game of paint ball. Another stand held our shields that we'd forged with Hephaistos. There was also a stable of a few animals. I spied the wings of a Pegasus as it stamped impatiently around the grounds.

The buzzing of voices filled the air, along with a bit of confusion, then the group split in two, half settling around Lucian, and the other around Revana. It didn't seem planned but just a natural separation.

Then Lucian just took charge, and I watched as everyone in our group turned their attention to him. I was pleased to see it, as he was a born leader. Deep down, there was a little dagger of envy stabbing me in the gut. I tried to bury it, angry at myself for its existence.

"We need to organize into two squads. One on the ground and the other in the air. We need those with good elemental skills on the ground. The best flyers should be in the air."

Georgina and Ren moved off to the side along with Marek.

"Jasmine, can you lead our ground troops?"

"Yes." Jasmine gave my hand a quick squeeze then moved over with them.

"Blue," Lucian said, nodding to me. "You're the best flyer here. You'll be with me, Quinn, and Hella."

I saluted him. "Aye, aye, Captain." Then I chuckled, but no one else laughed. I guess they didn't think I was funny. Lucian didn't crack a smile, either. Oops.

"Suit up then into formation."

While everyone went over to the armory to get their preferred weapon, I watched as Lucian made his way to talk to Revana. She'd arranged her group into similar squads. I hated that my gut churned at seeing them together. When Revana smiled at something Lucian said, my hands clenched into tight fists. Jealously was a bitch.

"You okay?" Jasmine asked, as she fastened a scabbard and sword to her back.

"Yup." I reached for a long bow and quiver of arrows.

Her brow furrowed. "You seem different."

"In what way?"

"You seem harder. Closed off." My eyebrows rose and I scowled as she added, "Defensive."

"I've been locked away for two months, Jas. My only companions have been the dark God of the Underworld and three bat-like women who take training to a whole other level of difficult."

Her eyes widened. "You've been training with the Furies?"

"Yup. They're as harsh as you've read about." I lifted my head to show her another scar on my neck to go with my lightning ones that I'd picked up along the way. I ran my fingers over it. "Courtesy of Allec, during weapons training. She likes to play with knives."

"I'm sorry, Mel." She wrapped her arms around

me and hugged me tight. It was a bit awkward, as the hilt of her sword nearly smacked me in the forehead.

"It's okay."

We broke apart when Lucian returned to grab a sword and back scabbard. He looked from me to her. "Everything all right?"

I nodded.

Another horn sounded, this one was louder and longer, and I suspected signaled the beginning of the melee. A wave of excitement and nerves rippled through the group. I found I was eager to get into the air and fight.

Lucian lifted his sword into the air. "Follow me!" His wings unfurled, and he flapped them a couple of times to stretch them out.

Thankful for the way my outfit was designed, my wings came out quickly and unhindered. I shot up into the air almost immediately. I hovered over the group, knowing full well I made a savage picture. Like a giant, black raven, a human-sized bird of prey. Lucian joined me in the air, as did Quinn and Hella.

I had to resist the urge to shoot forward and lead the charge, allowing Lucian to go first. I flew on his right side, Hella on his left, and Quinn brought up the rear. Down below, I saw Jasmine mounted on one of the giant, black fire horses, galloping across the field, the others, weapons drawn, running behind her. The scene nearly brought me to tears it was so powerful. She was glorious.

As we flew toward the rise before the woods, Revana and her squad of four flyers came alongside our formation. From below, I imagined we looked like two stealth jet fighters going in for the kill. Or at least, I hoped that's what we looked like.

I didn't know what to expect, but as we came over the rise, I gasped at what we encountered.

Helen of Troy flew up from the cover of the woods on the back of Pegasus. She had on gold armor and held a long bow much like mine. Beside her flew a giant in black armor and bull-like helmet. His gold wings extended the breadth of two of us. His sword glinted in the sunlight nearly blinding me.

"Veer right," Lucian shouted.

As one, we swerved right. I knocked an arrow and turned to fire while the others kept flying. I fired, aiming at Helen. I hit Pegasus with the blunted tip. The beast let out an angry snort, as red blossomed across its chest.

The rules of the game dictated that Helen had to drop to the ground as her mount was injured. I saw the fury on her face and heard the string of curses coming out of her mouth. I couldn't stop the bubble of laughter as I flew closer to her, nocking another arrow.

There were no referees in this game, so she could've stayed in the air and attacked me, but valor got the best of her, and after letting one of her own arrows go at me, she dropped to the ground. I easily dodged the arrow.

The demigod in the black armor swooped toward me. Lucian and the others flew up beside me just as his long sword made a dangerous arc at my face. I didn't have my shield, as it was too cumbersome to fly with so, I couldn't block the attack. I folded my wings in so I'd drop, but before I could act, the clang of metal reverberated in the air as Lucian's sword blocked the parlay, protecting me from injury. It was so loud it vibrated over my skin.

This gave me an opportunity to nock another arrow and let it fly. The demigod's armor deflected the arrow and didn't make a blood splatter, but it did make him think twice about attacking all four of us, and he spun away from us, his wings like razors cutting through the air.

I was about to pursue him when Lucian grabbed my arm. "We don't split up, Blue."

I shrugged his hand off. "He's retreating. We could bring him down if we all attacked him at once."

"Together, okay? That's how we'll win."

I nodded. "Sure. You're in charge."

He frowned, obviously not liking my tone of voice. But I couldn't keep my annoyance and frustration out of it. I had that guy in my sights. I knew I could take him on my own.

Together, we swooped down into the battle raging on the ground. I could see Georgina wrapping vines around a raging demigod who used her fire to burn away the plants just as fast. Ren had Heracles locked in a water tornado. Jasmine traded sword blows with Helen, who had replaced her bow and arrow with a short sword and shield.

I spotted a large, bare-chested man with huge curved horns sprouting from his head standing on the ridge, shooting arrows into the group. When he moved, I saw his bottom half was that of a goat, hooves and fur and all. I nocked an arrow and aimed it at him as I flew down toward the ground.

A high-pitched shriek drew my attention, as a fierce female warrior with spiked armored shoulder plates and long, flaming red hair flowing out from under a Trojan helmet shot through the air and ploughed Hella right in the back, knocking her down to the ground. Hella landed in a heap on a bunch of rocks. There wasn't any blood, but she definitely wasn't moving.

Stopping on a dime, I spun around, and nocking an arrow, I let it rip at the redhead. She smacked it away with her sword, letting out another shriek as she dove at me. I grinned, eager for a worthy challenge.

Lucian flew up to me. "We need to head toward the field. There's a break in ranks. Revana needs us there to protect the academy."

"But I can take this bitch out right here and now."

"Mel." His voice was filled with anger, which in turn made me angry. I really didn't need his lecture right now. "We need to work together as a team if we're going to win this battle."

"You guys go ahead and I'll catch up. This won't take me long."

Lucian shook his head but nodded to Quinn, and they flew off toward the field. Once they were gone, the redhead hovered closer to me.

"I'm Enyo," she said. "Goddess of War and Destruction."

"Melany. Human of rebellion and pissing people off."

She laughed. "I like your scars. They're very pretty."

"I like yours, too." She had white lines down her cheeks and down her arms, like tiger stripes.

"Each scar represents a kill I've made."

I did a quick count of the scars that I could see, and it came to more than fifty. She was trying to scare me. And maybe if I hadn't spent the last two months sparring with the Furies, the three most frightening women I'd ever met, I might have been.

"Good for you."

She grinned, and I saw that her teeth had been filed down into points. She looked like a shark. "You are the one who Hades chose."

"I guess."

"I can see why. You have an air of fearlessness."

"It's a gift." I shrugged.

She laughed. "Let's see how long that lasts." Lifting her sword, she flew toward me like a bullet.

My bow was ineffectual at this close range, so I let it

drop to the ground, and reaching around my waist, I unsheathed the two daggers I had strapped to my back underneath my cloak. I veered to the left and spinning to the side, I swiped my knives. One blade caught her across the arm.

I'd forgotten that my weapons weren't blunted. They were real lethal weapons made to wound, and blood ran in rivulets across her pale skin. Shocked, she hovered in midair and looked down at the gaping gash in her flesh.

"You will pay for that."

The horn sounded, ending the battle. I didn't know if it was because the enemy had breached our battle lines and reached the academy, or if I had been caught breaking the rules of combat.

Enyo folded her wings in, and she dropped to the ground. I watched as she landed, and the warrior in the black armor came to her side to inspect her wound. Others came to her as well, both demigod and my fellow cadets.

Lucian looked up at me. Even from here, I could see the disappointment on his face.

I floated down to the ground, folding my wings onto my back.

Everyone gathered around me but didn't come too close. I saw looks of anger and fear on some faces. Before I could catch it, gratification swelled in my chest at the terror I'd invoked. Allec, Tis, and Meg would be proud of me. I couldn't wait to return home to tell them.

Heracles pushed through the murmuring crowd toward me. "You broke the rules, Melany. You disqualified the entire group from the battle."

I glanced around at the faces staring at me. Jasmine and Georgina both looked at me like I was a monster. My stomach roiled at what I'd done. What the hell had come over me?

I shook my head, trying to cast off the clinging anger that seemed to be wrapping itself tighter and tighter around me.

"I'm... I don't... I'm sorry." I licked my lips, suddenly feeling sick.

"You risked getting expelled." His voice was low as he spoke to me. I could see he didn't want to punish me.

"I understand."

"Next time, you will be."

Revana stepped out of the group. "That's bullshit. She should be tossed out! Why are you always sticking up for her? She doesn't belong here. She's trash. Everyone knows it. Just look at her."

A savage heat flared in my chest and rushed over my limbs. Hatred, pure and blazing hot, filled me. All I could see was a red haze before my eyes. Before I could stop myself, my hand clenched into a fist, and I punched Revana in the face. Blood spewed from her nose as she stumbled sideways.

And Gods help me, but I liked seeing her bleed.

Gasps sounded all around me. I spotted Georgina's horrified face as she stared at me.

"Jesus, Mel." Jasmine's voice came from behind me.

I didn't turn around to face her. I couldn't.

I wrapped my hand over the amulet around my neck, stepped into a shadow on the ground, and vanished.

CHAPTER THIRTEEN

MELANY

J didn't know if it was my swirling mass of conflicted emotions that fueled my travel through the shadows, but I stepped out into the library in a matter of seconds. The trip was so quick, zipping through the ether, I ended up nauseated. I had to bend over and take in some deep breaths or vomit all over the nice, clean hardwood floor of Hades's library.

"Back so soon? I thought for sure I was going to have to come get you at the end of the day."

I glanced up as Hades strolled across the dimly lit room toward me, an air of extreme superiority wafting off him like too much cologne. He was haughty and entitled, behaving like he hadn't stolen me away against my will for two months, lying to me the entire time.

And in that moment, I hated him with every fiber of my being.

Hands ablaze with fire, I launched at him, trying to wrap those fiery appendages around his throat. But he was quick, and I suspected he had anticipated my attack. He dodged out of the way, as he pushed me to the side.

I stumbled into the drinks table, knocking over a decanter of water and two glasses. They shattered on the floor, sending shards of glass sliding across the wood. Water splashed over me and doused the fire from my hands. I turned and dove at him again, this time with electricity coiling around my fingers. One touch and I would shock him.

He dodged away from me again, this time pushing me into the wall. I bonked my head against the wood paneling, which just made me angrier. Incensed, I flung my hands toward him, intending to send a bolt of lightning at him, but the sparks fizzled, landing on the ground with little ping sounds. It was like one of those sparklers that people lit on birthday cakes or during the Fourth of July.

"I'm getting tired of this game." He cocked an eyebrow at me as if he was bored to tears with my outrage.

I glared at him, focusing on the shadows all around the room. I imagined them moving and swirling toward us. I pictured a rope of darkness twisting around Hades, squeezing. Squeezing until he couldn't move.

With a flick of his hand, a tendril of shadow coiled around me instead. It wrapped around my throat, my wrists and ankles, pulling tight, and I was flung backwards. I hit the wall, the back of my head hitting the wood hard enough I saw stars. I was yanked upwards until my feet dangled three feet off the ground.

Hades strolled across the room until he stood right in front of me. "I admire your spunk. It's one of the reasons I picked you. But did you really think you could use the shadows against me? I am the shadows, darling."

I struggled against the restraints on my arms and legs, but it was to no avail. I wasn't going anywhere until Hades decided to let me go. I was at his mercy. Again. Always.

"Why are you so angry?" he asked, and I heard a genuine interest to know.

"You've had me locked down here for two months!"

He nodded. "Ah. I see. I was sure I explained how time worked down here. Every day here is like two of them topside."

"You didn't explain it. You let me believe I'd only been here for a few weeks when in fact I've been gone for months."

He tapped his lips with a finger. "Hmm. I can understand why that would be upsetting. I apologize for not explaining the rules."

I glared at him some more, trying to muster up

some witty comeback, but I could feel my anger dissipating like mist in the morning sunshine.

"Is there anything else you wish to yell at me about? You might as well get it all out in one fell swoop. It's not good to bottle these things up. I heard it can cause stress related illness."

I knew he was making fun of me. It was in his tone and the way he tilted his head to regard me with a slight upturn at the side of his mouth, like a parent indulging a child having a rip-roaring tantrum.

I sagged into the shadows pinning me up against the wall. There wasn't any more point to fighting. Hades was too strong; I was never going to win. Besides that, I wasn't entirely sure I wanted to hurt him. Maybe I'd just wanted that apology he gave. Some acknowledgement that this situation sucked for me.

With a wave of his hand, the shadow bonds evaporated, and I dropped to the floor. I put out my hand to brace against the wall, so I didn't fall onto my knees. He reached for me. I shied away from his hand, but he persisted and grabbed my arm and led me to one of the chairs in front of the giant fireplace. A fire crackled pleasantly inside. Heat washed over me.

He poured two glasses of wine, set it on the table between the chairs, and then sat in the other chair. "Now, tell me what's really upsetting you."

Sinking into the chair, I smirked. "As if you care."

"Of course I care, Melany. You're important to me."

I looked at him wondering if that was really true. He met my gaze, and I wasn't one hundred percent sure what I saw in the dark depths. Could a God like Hades truly care? About the world? About me? I wanted it to be true because at the moment, I felt truly alone.

"I think the others are scared of me." I was surprised by my confession. It wasn't something I was sure I could talk about, especially not with him.

"Of course they are." He picked up one of the glasses of wine and took a sip, watching me over the rim. "You're fierce. You're strong. You're better trained. They'd be stupid to not fear you."

I was startled to find his compliments pleased me. I picked up the other wine glass and took a sip. The second the wine hit my tongue, my stomach growled, reminding me I hadn't eaten since breakfast.

Hades smiled. "Shall we eat?"

I returned his smile.

In the dining hall, the little wooden robots served us roasted duck and a warm beet salad. At first I wasn't too sure about the meal, but after the first few bites my taste buds were in heaven. I finished it all in record time, which made Hades chuckle.

"I like that you have such a hearty appetite. A lot of young women worry so needlessly about overeating. It's stupid. Food, drink… these things should be enjoyed."

I eyed him across the table, wondering if there were a few other things that should be enjoyed that he purposely left out. Maybe it was inappropriate of me to consider those things, but I couldn't help it. Hades piqued several of my interests.

"Did you eat like this when you lived at the Demos estate?"

The question took me by surprise, and I nearly dropped my fork that was halfway to my mouth. I hadn't realized he knew anything about me besides I'd passed the twelve trials, a feat no one else had ever achieved in the history of the academy.

"Don't look surprised. Of course I know everything about you."

"Why?"

"I don't invest in something that I don't know anything about. So I did my research on you." He sat back in his chair. "Melany Richmond, eighteen, parents Andrew and Joanna Richmond, orphaned at age three and a half, lived in an orphanage until the age of thirteen when your mother's estranged sister, Sophie, found you and adopted you. You came to live on the Demos estate where Sophie worked... I imagine living with Callie Demos was hellish. I bet she was furious when her shadowbox contained nothing but a simple birthday message and not the invitation she'd been expecting." He chuckled to himself. "Such a vain girl."

My heart squeezed painfully at the mention of my adopted mother, and I threw my napkin onto my plate. "I don't want to hear anymore."

"I know what happened to her."

My eyes narrowed, and I glared at him. The image of the pale hand I saw in the rubble of the guest house still haunted my dreams. I'd worked hard at diminishing the pain of that moment; I didn't need it brought up all over again to torture me.

"She died in an earthquake," I said through gritted teeth.

"Are you sure it was an earthquake?"

"I saw it. I saw the damage it did to the estate."

"Did you ever think it was odd that there was an earthquake in Pecunia?"

I had thought it was strange at the time. I'd questioned it even. There was no fault line near that part of the country. I'd found that piece of gold rope at the site of all that destruction. I'd mentioned it to Zeus and was basically electrocuted nearly to death for it.

He stood and walked over to my side of the table. He pulled out the chair next to me and sat. "You know what I'm talking about."

I frowned. "I'm not sure I do."

"Someone released one of the Titans from Tartarus. Probably Atlas." He waved a hand. "He likes to dig in the dirt."

I leaned toward him. "Why would someone do that? And who would do that?"

"Why does anyone do anything? For power, of course." He rubbed a finger over his lips. "You found that piece of golden rope?"

I nodded.

"The golden rope controls whoever or whatever it's wrapped around. And it could only come from one person…"

I knew the name he was going to speak before he said it. I'd had my suspicions from day one of being at the academy.

"Aphrodite."

"She's totally in cahoots with Ares," I blurted.

Hades's eyes narrowed. "I know they're having an affair and have been for centuries, but what do you mean 'in cahoots?'"

"The first night at the academy, I saw them sneaking around the halls, and I heard her mention something about a key, stealing it or something."

Pressing his lips together, Hades nodded. "Just as I suspected."

"Why would they release a Titan? Why destroy Pecunia and those other towns?"

"I suspect it was a test run for something bigger."

"Like what?"

"That I don't know." His lips lifted into a sly smile. "Yet."

"How are you going to find out?"

He pointed at me. "You're going to find out. I've taught you how to travel through the shadows. You can use them to move around the academy. You can get into places that I can't."

I shook my head. "They'll see me. It's not like I'm invisible."

"But you can be."

"How?"

"I'll show you." He stood and offered his hand to me. I took it, and he pulled me to my feet. My skin tingled where he touched me. Licking my lips, unsure if I liked that feeling, I tugged my hand away and rubbed it against my leg. It did nothing to diminish the pleasant sensation of touching him.

I followed him out of the dining hall, across the expanse of the corridor, and into his personal suite. He led me to the far wall where a six-foot high painting dominated the space. It depicted a nearly naked, muscular man with longish black hair and a rigid face. He had horns curling from the sides of his head and fire shooting from his mouth. On the ground, cowering in front of him was a beautiful young woman with long black hair and pale skin, wearing a long blue dress. It slipped down to reveal her shoulder. It was a powerful picture, and it made me shiver.

"I don't think the artist did me much justice. I look like I should be in an eighties hair band."

I glanced at Hades as he gazed up at the painting.

"Mind you, it was a different time then. I was a different guy in the 1500s." He chuckled. "And no matter what you're thinking, I definitely didn't pose for that. The artist took a lot of liberties. I haven't breathed fire in a millennia."

"Who's the woman?"

"No one you know."

The look on his face darkened; he obviously didn't want to discuss it. So I stopped asking questions.

He slid his hand along the frame of the painting, and then he pulled it forward, like opening a door. Behind it, imbedded in the wall was a metal door. It looked like a safe, with a numbered knob and a metal crank.

Hades spun the knob to the right, then to the left, then to the right again. He pulled on the lever, but the safe didn't open. Frowning, he tried the combination again, but it still didn't unlock.

He sighed, and then shouted, "Charon!"

Seconds later, the decrepit-looking butler floated into the room. "Yes, my Lord."

"What is the Gods damned combo? You didn't change it on me, did you?"

"Of course not, my Lord." Charon reached for the knob, flicked it quickly one way then the other. He cranked on the lever; there was a distinctive clicking sound, and he pulled the safe door open.

"Ah, thank you, Charon."

The butler tipped his skull-head and then floated out of the room.

"Why didn't you just snap your fingers and open it? What's the point of being a God if you can't just snap things into existence?"

He shrugged. "Where's the fun in that? After a few thousand years, things like that get boring. Besides that, Hephaistos forged this for me with special metal to prevent something like that happening. No one can open this without the combo. Not even me, obviously." He chuckled.

"But what if Charon hadn't been here? What would you have done?"

"Charon is always here. Even death hasn't stopped him." Hades pulled the door wide open. Inside the safe sat a horned helmet made from the blackest of metals. The front face plate had openings for the eyes and mouth, and a nose guard only. And it sported horns that were similar to that of a big horned sheep. He reached in and drew it out. "It's called the Helm of Darkness." He set it on top of his head.

In an instant, he vanished from sight.

I stared at the spot he'd been in then swung around searching for him, anxious that he would pop up behind me and scare me. I heard his distinctive chuckle next to me, and then I felt a slight brush of air on my cheek as he moved positions. Curious, I raised my hand to touch him, my fingers brushing up against the metal of the helm covering his face.

Then he reappeared in front of me as he removed the helmet and set it under his arm. "Ta da. Pretty cool, right?"

I snickered. "Yeah, it's cool." I reached for it. "Can I try it on?"

He pulled it away from my grasp. "No."

"Then why show it to me?" I shook my head as I turned to leave. "You're frustrating, you know that?"

"I showed it to you, so you know what it looks like when you make your own."

"What do you mean when I make my own? I can't make something like that."

"Sure you can. You made your shield. One of the best ones from what Hephaistos says."

Frowning, I studied him. "He said that?" I found that almost impossible to believe. Hephaistos didn't do praise. He was the sternest, grumpiest man I'd ever met.

Hades nodded. "He likes you."

I pulled a face. "Bullshit. Hephaistos doesn't like anyone."

"He didn't smack you with a hammer, did he?"

"No."

"And he worked with you after class, didn't he?"

"I suppose." I shrugged.

"Then he likes you."

I still wasn't so sure that meant he liked me. Tolerated was more like it. "He's not going to let me come into his forge to make an invisibility helmet. I mean, where do I even start? Does he know how to make one? Who made that for you?"

"Brontes, a cyclops who was a good friend way back when. Brontes and his brothers taught Hephaistos how to forge, so I'm sure he has the knowledge."

"And why would he even help me?"

"Because Hephaistos has a stake in this. I mean, Aphrodite is his wife, and she's been cheating on him for hundreds of years. And I know he detests Ares. Who doesn't, honestly?"

"Then why hasn't he just divorced her?"

"Because divorce is the mortal way of doing things. We Gods… we get revenge instead." He grinned, and that fire inside his eyes ignited.

CHAPTER FOURTEEN

MELANY

*O*ver the next couple days while I trained, I thought about what Hades wanted me to do. Sneak back into the academy and spy on the other Gods. But first I had to sneak into the forge and make myself an invisibility helmet. I didn't know why I couldn't just borrow his. I mean, it wasn't like he was using it. When I brought it up the next evening at dinner, he refused to answer and just changed the subject, preferring to discuss how social media was making people stupid.

I considered just ignoring his request. It wasn't like he could make me do it, but he knew I would, anyway. Hades knew I wanted to find out who was responsible for Sophie's death and make them pay. Revenge was an exceptional motivator.

But it was also a distraction, and I got hit in the shoulder by Allecto's sword during training. The blade wasn't blunted, but thankfully I wore light armor or else my arm probably would've been dangling from my side as I bled out all over the floor.

"Where's your head, girl?"

I shook it, trying to clear it, so next time I didn't get a sword through the gut. "Sorry."

"Sorry?" She sneered. "Sorry is for cowards and weaklings. Are you a coward or a weakling?"

"No."

"Then quit acting like it." She took a few steps back and raised her sword. "Let's go again."

I shook my head again, rolled my shoulders, then went into my defensive stance, my sword lifted and ready to parry.

I trained with Allecto for another hour and then did flying tactics with Tisiphone. After that, Megaera put me through my paces through the obstacle course over and over again until my legs were rubber, and my abdominals quivered from exertion. Honestly, it felt like I'd been punched in the gut with an iron fist repeatedly.

After eating, Hades was noticeably absent. I sat in my room and paced. I couldn't relax, despite training for eight hours. I had too many thoughts about the supposed earthquake that killed Sophie. What if what Hades had said was true, and that Aphrodite and Ares were somehow responsible? What if they were planning something else? I had to do something.

Dressing in my best stealthy black clothes, I stood in my room and concentrated on the shadows lurking in every corner. I gathered them to me, pictured the door outside of Hephaistos's forge, and then dissolved into the darkness to make the trip.

It wasn't as long or hard as my first trip to the dining hall, but it still had its problems. I'd almost gotten lost and ended up walking out into the crowded corridor near the dining hall. I'd heard Jasmine's voice, so it was really difficult not to just walk out of the shadows instead. I wanted to explain to her about what had happened before, about the anger that seemed to be growing inside of me. But I wasn't sure she'd understand. I didn't fully understand.

When I materialized right outside the forge, I was thankfully alone. It was late, so I didn't think anyone would be inside working. Not any of my fellow cadets, anyway. I crept inside, the heat of the fires blowing over me. It never failed to literally take my breath away. It was as if all the oxygen in my lungs was being sucked out to feed the flames.

I moved across the room, over the bridge, and up to the main forge. The bellows pumped hard keeping the fire high and hot. I didn't know exactly what I was planning to do. I mean, how the hell did a person create an invisibility helmet? But Hades had told me there should be a mold there and the right type of metal. After that, all it needed to work was a piece of shadow weaved into it. Hades said he'd show me how to do that.

I found where Hephaistos stacked the clay molds. I discovered a mold for an ax blade and a mace, and then I found one for what looked like a war helmet. I took it and placed it on the forging table. I needed to pour molten metal into it.

I went to the storage units and found a hunk of black metal that appeared similar to what Hades's helm was made from. Now, how the heck did I get it over to the mold? Thinking back to my time in the forge when we made our shields, I remembered how Hephaistos moved the giant blocks of metal around with ropes and pulleys. I looked up to see a contraption hanging above the storage units.

I hooked it up to the hunk of metal then using the ropes, I raised it up and pulled it along the track on the ceiling to the table across the forge. As the block of metal hung over the mold, I realized I didn't know what the hell I was doing. I should've taken the metal to the tank to be melted then used the gutters to transport it to the mold. But I didn't have that kind of time. I had to be innovative.

I lifted my hands and flicked my fingers back and forth until flames erupted. I focused on the fire until it was so hot, it turned blue-white. Hoping for the best, I set my hands onto the hunk of metal and coaxed the flames higher. It took a few minutes, but eventually the metal began to melt, and it dripped down into the mold. Although some of it didn't quite make it into the mold. There were globs of metal all over the table and floor.

"What are you doing to my forge, girl!"

I swung around to see Hephaistos, huge hammer in his hand, glaring at me.

"Um, making a helmet."

He limped over to the table to see what I was doing. His scowl deepened. "You're making a mess and destroying my work station."

I really examined what I'd done and he was right. Sort of. I was definitely making a mess, but I didn't think I'd destroyed the table. I might've burned some holes into it with my molten metal, but I was sure it could be repaired.

He picked up the mold, glaring at me. "Did Hades put you up to this? Did he tell you to come wreak some havoc in my forge?"

I shook my head vehemently. Hephaistos never really scared me in the past. I'd always thought of him as some old, frail God past his prime, but I realized right there and then he could've ended me if he wanted to. Despite his weathered and aged appearance, he was still a God with fire at his disposal in a blink of an eye.

"I'm trying to make a helmet for myself."

His eyes narrowed. "What kind of helmet?"

"A helm of darkness, like the one Hades has."

"Why in the blazes do you need a helmet like that?"

"To be invisible." Then it all came pouring out. I told him about the earthquake and about seeing my adopted mother buried in the rubble and about what Hades had told me about it not being natural—that someone had released a Titan to do the dirty work. I kept Aphrodite's involvement out of it, for now. I had a feeling that despite her cheating ways he still loved her.

"You know you can't believe everything Hades tells you. He can be manipulative and conniving. There's a reason why he was banned from the academy until now."

"Yeah? And why was that?"

He gave me a long look and then dropped his gaze, busying himself with cleaning up the mess I'd made. "It's complicated. He has a long and arduous relationship with his brothers. Especially Zeus."

"I figured as much, but it doesn't matter to me. All I care about is finding out who killed Sophie. If someone in this academy is responsible, I want to know."

"And if you find out, what are you going to do about it?"

I shrugged. "I don't know yet. But something has to be done."

"I don't think it's going to be as easy as that."

"We're training here to be in an army to protect the people of the Earth, aren't we?"

He didn't say anything.

"Then that's what I'm trying to do. I want to protect those people from future situations. What if what Hades says is true? And that earthquake was just a test for something bigger, something nastier."

He sighed, shaking his head. "I'll make the helmet for you. It won't be as fancy as Hades's, but it will work the same."

I perked up. "You will? Why?"

"Because I sense you want to do the right thing. That's a rare quality, especially in someone so young."

I resisted the urge to embrace him, knowing he'd hate it and would probably shove me away. "Thank you." I hung my head. "You might be the only one who thinks that about me right now."

"But be careful, girl. There is a lot going on in this place that you have no clue about. Not everything is as it seems and that includes Hades. I don't think he means you any harm, but he's not your friend. You are a means to an end for him, despite what he tells you or tries to make you believe."

I didn't want to believe that. I felt something spark between me and Hades. I wasn't sure exactly what it was. Friendship? Probably not. Attraction? For me, yes, although I'd been trying to fight it. And for him? He did look at me differently lately. Sometimes, I'd catch him watching me, when he thought I hadn't noticed. But I had. His gaze was potent and would sometimes make me shiver. More nights than I cared to admit, I had dreams about him.

I pushed the thoughts away as I concentrated on what Hephaistos asked me to do. Together, we cleaned up the mess I'd made and started the process over again. This time the right way. By the time I travelled the shadows back to my room in Hades Hall, I was exhausted.

I stripped out of my clothes, as they stunk of fire and burned metal, put on my pajamas, and climbed into bed. But before I could close my eyes, the alarm bell started to clang. It was time for me to get up and get ready for another long day of training.

Sighing, I rolled over onto my side and crammed a pillow over my head. I wasn't moving. Hades was going to have to come in here and yank me out of this bed by my leg. I wouldn't put it past him to do just that. But until then, I shut my eyes in protest. I was going to get some damn sleep even if it killed me.

CHAPTER FIFTEEN

MELANY

*A*fter Hades found out I'd gone to the forge to make my own invisibility helmet, he loosened the chains binding me to the hall and allowed me to return to the academy to do some more group training. I was equal parts excited and nervous. What if my friends didn't want to see me again after what I'd done? What if Lucian didn't feel the same way about me anymore? I couldn't just pop back into their lives like last time; I needed to ease my way in gradually. So instead of appearing in the middle of the dining hall like a rock star, I opted to humbly walk back in through the front doors.

But first, I decided on a little detour to get my mind right.

I emerged from the shadows into the center of the giant hedge maze. I took in a deep, greedy breath of fresh, cool air. Being underground all the time was hard on the lungs. I raised my face to the light shining down. I hadn't realized how much I missed sunlight until now. When I got back to the hall, I was going to ask Hades for one of those light therapy lamps, so I didn't get depressed.

When I stepped out of the gazebo, I thought I was alone, so I was surprised when I spied a lone figure sitting on one of the stone benches next to one of the statues of a male soldier brandishing a spear and holding a shield. I was stunned to see Medusa leaning back, her long legs stretched out in front of her, with her arms spread out along the back of the bench, her face raised to the sun. She didn't wear sunglasses and had her white eyes wide open.

I suspected I was intruding on a private moment, so I quickly turned to jump back into the shadows, but my foot accidentally crunched a small twig. The cracking sound was like a bullhorn in the relative silence of the maze.

"Trying to sneak away?"

I stopped and turned back. "I didn't want to disturb you."

"Too late." She blinked at me with those stark white eyes and then slid on her dark sunglasses. "Hades let you out, I see."

I didn't know how to answer that so I just nodded.

"I heard what you did to Enyo the other day." She smirked.

"It was an accident," I heard myself say, knowing full well that was bullshit.

She shrugged. "I'm the last person who's going to judge you. Everyone makes mistakes. Some mistakes are just more severe than others." Her head titled up to the stone statue beside the bench.

Her sympathy surprised me. "Thanks."

She got to her feet, towering over me by a foot at least. "Oh don't mistake me. We're not friends. And if you ever did to me what you did to Enyo, you wouldn't be breathing. You'd be as solid as this guy next to me." She turned to leave, her snake hair lifted up to hiss at me, one of the little vipers even snapped its jaws, and then she disappeared into the maze.

Despite her threat, I felt buoyed by what Medusa had said. People made mistakes. I'd made one. Surely, my friends would forgive me for it. I left the maze and went into the academy through the main doors.

The hallways buzzed with activity. Heads turned and conversations stopped when I was spotted. I didn't let it get to me. Instead, I streamed along with them, looking for a friendly face. I spotted Georgina up ahead. I jogged to catch up to her.

"Gina."

She spun around, her eyes wide. "Mel?" She

jumped and hugged me. "Oh my Gods, we all thought we wouldn't see you again."

"What? Why?"

"I don't know. You just disappeared."

"I was ashamed of what I did to Enyo. I didn't think you'd want to see me again."

She hugged me again. "Are you kidding? We've been missing you badly."

People walked quickly around us. A couple of them eyed me with suspicion.

"Where is everyone going?"

"Weapons training on the field with Ares and Heracles."

"Can I come with you?"

She smiled and grabbed my hand. "Of course. Jas and Ren and Lucian are going to be so excited to see you."

Together, we pushed through the crowd out the side door and onto the training field. I spotted Lucian instantly. He was standing at the front of the group helping to organize cadets into various training squads.

His gaze met mine and he smiled. All my nervousness and doubt melted away when I saw that radiant grin. Seeing him like this, being here out in the open, made me realize just how much I missed the light. Obviously, in more ways than one.

I walked toward him. "Do you have room for one more?"

I heard the whispers around me. "I can't believe she came back after what she did."

"Why does Lucian even like her?"

"She should be kicked out."

Lucian met me halfway and pulled me into his arms. I sighed into his chest, inhaling him. Gods, I'd missed him. I missed this level of human contact. I'd been yelled at, chased, smacked, sparred with, insulted, pushed for long enough, that I'd forgotten what a simple hug felt like and how much I needed it.

"Gods Blue, don't disappear like that again." He nuzzled his face into my neck.

"I'll try not to but I can't promise."

When he drew back and looked me in the eyes, I sensed he wanted to kiss me. If we were in private, I knew he would have.

"Break it up." Ares marched across the field glowering at us. "It's time for training." He pointed at me. "You line up with the other spearmen. I want to see if you've gotten any better."

I did as he suggested, grabbing a spear from the weapons rack, and then got in the front line along with ten other cadets, including Mia and Revana. Revana gave me the nastiest look I'd ever seen, and I hoped I had a chance to wipe it off her face.

Ares stood in front of us and then counted off. "One, two, three, four, five." Then he started counting again. "One, two, three, four, five. Now, line up and face off against each other."

We all moved into our positions and as luck would
have it, I faced off against Revana. The Gods smiled
down on me today, and I couldn't stop the grin blossoming across my face. I was very pleased to see that
my smile made her nervous.

"I've been waiting for this for a long time," she said.

"Me too."

Ares raised his arm in the air and then brought it
down. "Begin!"

I took a step back, the spear in both hands, and
then spun it around like a windmill. Allecto had shown
me how to do it. It was a display of aggression and skill,
and I loved how wide Revana's eyes got when I spun it
over my head, around my back, and then ended it with
a grunt, in a side squat with the spear thrust out across
my waist. I straightened then brought the spear back to
my side in the ready position.

I was showing off, but I couldn't help it. From day
one, this girl had thought she was better than me. She'd
gone out of her way to bully me, insult me, and do
everything in her power to put me down. She would've
had me kicked out of the academy, which would have
made me one of the lost—I'd be a person without
memory of this place, my friends, or my family—if
she'd had her way.

I owed this girl nothing. Not even my mercy.

So when she thrust her spear at me, thinking she
could spar with me, that somehow she was even in the

same league as I was, I knocked it away, spun, and had the tip of my spear pressed against her neck. Just like that, I had bested her. If this had been a real battle, out on the field, it would've taken me no more than a minute to end her life.

The tip of the spear was blunted, so I couldn't jab her through the neck but I wanted to. I could feel the bloodlust rising up inside of me. Megaera spoke in a low whisper against my ear, "She's not worthy to be called a warrior. You're better than she is. She's had it good her whole life while you suffered." Tisiphone's voice was low and seductive in my mind. "She wants you to fail. She wants you to suffer. She's trying to turn Lucian against you. She's trying to steal him for her own. You can't let her win." Allecto's voice was the loudest of them all. "Kill her. Kill her now!"

After pulling my spear back from her throat, I swept her leg, and she fell onto her back on the ground. I spun my spear over my head again and then thrust it forward. Ares snatched the pole away from me before I could jab her in the gut with the blunted tip.

"It's done. You won. Time to walk away."

I raised my head and stared Ares in the eyes. An uncontrollable fury surged through me and I wanted to lash out at him, but I couldn't show my hand like that. Not yet. Not until I had proof. "You're the one who should walk away."

He met my gaze, and it was hard and menacing,

but I didn't back down. I was never going to back down ever again.

"You've been in the Underworld too long, cadet. You're starting to say some crazy stuff."

I opened my mouth to fling an accusation his way, but Lucian was beside me, guiding me off the field.

When we were alone, he sighed and shook his head. "What is going on with you? This isn't you. You're out of control."

Anger still swirled around in my belly, but it was starting to fade. I took in a few deep breaths and tried to clear the bloodlust from my mind. Every once in a while, it flashed like a strobe light. In the light were visions of blood and chaos and mayhem. And I had caused it.

I glanced down at my hands and swore I saw they were painted red with blood.

Lucian grabbed them. "Tell me what's going on. Why go after Revana like that?"

"She deserved it. She's a horrible person."

"We all know that, but we're supposed to be on the same side. We have to be able to trust each other, not turn on one another."

I shook my head, trying to clear my thoughts. "Since when did you stick up for Revana? Are you two friends again?"

He sighed. "No, we're not friends, but we've learned to work together."

I didn't say anything about that. I hated that it

made me jealous to even consider that they could be friends.

"And what did you say to Ares? I've never seen him that intense before, which is saying something."

"Someone killed Sophie."

His frown deepened. "It was an earthquake, Blue. You saw it."

I shook my head. "Someone released a Titan to destroy my town."

"You think Ares did that?"

"Aphrodite. Ares. Both of them. All of them." I shook my head and put my hands over my face. "I don't know. I'm confused."

"What is Hades doing to you down there?"

Instead of speaking, I just lunged into his arms. I buried my face in his chest and squeezed my eyes shut against the wave of anguish threatening to surge over me. Threatening to drown me in its violent deluge.

"Just hold me. Please, just hold me."

He did. He wrapped his arms around me and held me tight. He nuzzled his face against my head and whispered that everything was going to be okay, that he was there for me. The anger and hate started to dissipate as I anchored to him. He was my rock. My safe place. I had to remember that so I didn't dive off the edge.

Something was wrong with me. That much I knew. But I didn't know how to stop it. I was changing, morphing into someone else, something else. I was scared of what it was. But what was worse was that I wanted it to happen. I craved it. Because whatever was happening to me made me stronger, smarter, better. I knew it. And soon enough, the others would know it, too.

CHAPTER SIXTEEN

MELANY

*L*ucian and I didn't spend too much time together, as he had to get back to the training field. He wanted to stay with me, but I told him to go. I opted to leave while I still could. Every time I got around the others, something happened to me. I got enraged. All I wanted to do was fight and hurt people. It was obvious group training wasn't going to work for me any longer. Hades would be happy about that.

Although I didn't want to train with the others, that didn't mean I wanted to return to the hall. So I decided to check in at the forge to see if my helmet was finished. Hephaistos had told me it would take a few days for him to hammer it into submission.

Since everyone was outside in the training field, I had the halls of the academy to myself. I decided this was the perfect time to practice my stealth skills. When I heard the footsteps of someone approaching, I slunk into the shadows and stayed hidden.

Two students ran by the first time. Neither of them noticed me lurking along the wall shrouded in darkness. When they were gone, I stepped out again and continued on my way down to the forge. Right before I reached the stairs leading down into the bowels of the academy, I heard voices coming my way. I gathered the shadows to me like a cloak and hid underneath it.

Demeter and Dionysus came around the corner deep in conversation.

"I heard she attacked another person," Dionysus said.

Demeter gave him a discerning look. "We both know it isn't her fault."

"You have a soft spot for her," Dionysus said.

"I know. She reminds me so much of—"

"She's even starting to look like her. I imagine he's outfitted her entire wardrobe to his liking." They stopped walking, halting in the hall close to where I hid. Dionysus took out a metal flask from the inside pocket of his jacket, opened it, and took a sip. He handed it to Demeter. She took it and chugged a drink.

"I wish I could tell Melany that she has friends here in the academy." She handed the flask back to Dionysus, her gaze sweeping over where I was cloaked. "That she could talk to me if she needed to."

"You worry too much. She won't end up like Persephone."

"I hope you're right."

They moved on down the corridor. Once they turned to the left and disappeared, I came out of the shadows. It was obvious they'd been talking about me, but I didn't know what they'd meant about my attack on Revana not being my fault. And who the hell was Persephone? Was it the young woman who had been in the painting on Hades's wall in his suite?

I had a lot of questions for Hades when I returned to the hall, but right now I needed to see if my helmet of darkness was ready for me. I descended the stairs and pushed open the giant doors to Hephaistos's foundry. I crossed the floor, up the stone stairs, across the bridge arching over the rivers of molten metal, and then up to the main forge.

Hephaistos was there, striking his hammer against a red-hot glowing blade of steel. He stopped when he saw me and then dunked the raw new sword into a bucket of water. It hissed as steam billowed from the bucket. He pushed his goggles up onto his malformed head.

"I wondered when you would be back."

"I came for my helmet. Is it done?"

He set the hammer and pincers down onto the table and then moved over to the shelves behind the main forge. It was the place he kept the shadowboxes he made. I followed him over. He grabbed the black helmet on one of the shelves and handed it to me.

I grinned with pleasure. It was beautiful, sleek and not bulky like Hades's. The front plate dipped down over the forehead, but there was a butterfly-shaped opening for my eyes, nose, and mouth. Etched into the side plates were wisps of feathers. It looked like wings sprouted from the sides.

I ran my fingers over the carvings. "It's spectacular, Hephaistos. It's better than anything I could have ever hoped for."

My compliment seemed to please him, as he puffed up his chest. "You always reminded me of a bird. A hawk maybe, or a falcon. And when I heard you'd sprouted black wings instead of white, it didn't surprise me." He tapped the helmet with his finger. "Put it on. See how it fits."

I slid it over my head. It fit snugly, but not too tight. It was perfect. "How do I look?" I purposely unfurled my wings and spread them out around me. My shadow cut an impressive image on the stone floor.

Hephaistos took a step back. I didn't know if it was because my wings were taking up too much room, or he saw something that startled him. "You look all right." He moved back to his work. "Time for you to go. I'm busy."

I took the helmet off and followed him back to the

forge. "Hey, what do you know about someone named Persephone?"

His scowl deepened. "Where did you hear that name?"

"I heard it around. Who is she?"

"She's not your concern. I suggest you head back to the Underworld and quit asking dangerous questions."

"I think she's the woman I saw in one of Hades's paintings."

"Go away now." He picked up the long steel piece that was going to make an impressive sword and set it back into the hot coals.

"Do I look like her? Is that why Hades picked me?"

Hephaistos sighed then looked at me. "I don't perceive to know why Hades does anything. But what I do know, girl, is that you need to be careful. Protect yourself."

I resigned myself in the knowledge that he wasn't going to tell me anything. I nodded a goodbye, wrapped my hand over the amulet around my neck, and returned to Hades Hall.

The second I appeared in the corridor, I marched over to the library and went inside. Hades wasn't there sitting by the fire as he usually did, so I stomped down the hall to his suite. The door was shut.

Carefully, I turned the knob, pushing the door open and entered. On first look, the room was empty. The drapes were drawn on the big canopied bed, and Hades wasn't lying there, thank the Gods. I crept over to the big painting on the wall and looked up at it. I studied the woman on the ground, searching for a resemblance. It was hard to tell from a painting, as some things could've been distorted, but the shape of her face was a little familiar.

Setting my helmet down, I went over to the bookshelves on the far wall. Maybe there was something that could tell me who this woman was and her significance. I pawed through books, finding nothing. There were a couple of decorative boxes on the shelf. I opened them to find them empty. I pulled open one of the drawers to find a stack of rolled scrolls each tied with a red ribbon.

I took one out. I knew I shouldn't read his private correspondence; it was a huge breach in trust, but I had to know what was going on, so I slid the ribbon off and unrolled the parchment. The writing was cursive and flowy and very feminine.

My dearest…

I quickly perused the letter, a few names jumped out at me: Demeter, Aphrodite, Zeus. Then I looked down at the bottom to read…

Always yours,

Persephone

I was going to go back and start the letter again and really read it when the door opened and Hades came in. Startled, I tried to shove the letter back into the drawer, but I wasn't fast enough.

"What are you doing?"

"Who's Persephone?"

He strode toward me, his eyes flashing with fire. He snatched the letter from me, rolled it back up, and put the ribbon around it.

"Who's Persephone? Is that her in the painting?"

He put the scroll back into the drawer then pinned me with a hard look. "How dare you invade my privacy."

Frightened, I said, "I'm sorry, but I need to know who she is, and I knew you wouldn't tell me if I just asked."

"Well, we'll never know now, will we?"

"Please, I have a right to know."

He smirked. "A right to know? What makes you think you have any rights here?"

"People are saying I look like her. That you're dressing me up like her."

His eyes narrowed as he clenched his jaw. "What people?"

"I heard Demeter mention it. And I saw her name in the letter, so she must know the truth."

He glowered. "Demeter wouldn't know the truth if it bit her in the ass." He took me by the arm and started to pull me toward the door. "Get out of my room."

"Who is she? Obviously, it was someone you loved. I deserve to know, especially since—"

He whirled on me, his eyes flashing. "Since what?

Because you quickly read some random letter you think you know anything?"

His hand still gripping my arm, he backed me up into the wall. My hip hit the drinks table along the way. He loomed over me with a heated menace that brushed over my skin and made me shiver. My heart thudded hard in my chest. My lungs burned with each rapid breath I took. He was so close to me I could feel his hot breath against my cheek.

"N-n-no," I stammered.

"No, what?"

"No, I don't know anything."

His lips twitched upwards slyly. "Do you think because you might have a resemblance to her and I loved her, that I have feelings for you? Do you have some school girl crush on me, is that it?"

I shook my head so hard my hair flew around my face.

"Oh, I think maybe that's the truth." He leaned in closer to me. "I can hear your heart going pitty pat just thinking about it. I imagine your belly clenches in anticipation of what I might do to you. Right here. Right now." He reached with his hand and lightly encircled me around the waist. I took in a ragged breath.

I lifted my hand and set it on his chest, intending to shove him away, but I didn't. I left it there. I felt his heart racing under my palm. Panting hard, he licked his lips. His gaze raked my face, lingering on my mouth.

Oh my Gods, I couldn't breathe. It was too hot in the room. The air was thick and cloying. I should've pushed him back and gotten out of there, but the truth was I didn't want to move. I wanted him to do something. Anything. To put me out of my misery.

Then he crushed his mouth against mine. The kiss was hot and hard and frantic. Nothing like the gentle, loving kisses I'd shared with Lucian. No, this was all heat and passion and anger. Every nerve ending in my body flared to life.

Then it was over and he pulled back. My lips tingled from his absence.

"Persephone was a strong, smart, spectacular woman. She was the woman of my dreams. And you… are nothing like her." He took a couple of steps back and turned away.

It was a punch to the gut. I'd never felt anything as acutely as I did those words. Tears pricked the side of my eyes, but I wouldn't let them fall. He didn't deserve to witness my pain.

"Leave your helmet. I'll infuse it with shadow to make it work. Then you can do what I told you to do." He waved his hand toward the door. "You can go now. And if I ever find you in my room again, Melany, you will be punished. And it will hurt."

Swallowing, I pushed away from the wall and ran out of his room. I fled to mine, shut and locked the door, and then leaned back against it. Tears pushed past my eyelids and rolled down my cheeks. I'd been so foolish thinking Hades felt anything for me. I was obviously a means to an end for him. He didn't look at me like a woman; he only saw a solider, an instrument in whatever plot he was brewing. I knew that now. And I wouldn't let my guard down again.

CHAPTER SEVENTEEN

MELANY

*D*espite having a terrible sleep with horrific nightmares, I threw myself into my training the next day. I did the twenty-five pullups, fifty pushups, and hundred crunches without complaint. I ran ten laps around the arena and did the obstacle course three times without being prodded to do so.

When I suited up for combat sparring in silence, Allecto was in my face. "What's wrong with you?"

"What do you mean? I'm getting ready to spar with you."

"Yeah, but you're doing it without some pithy remark or sarcasm. So something must be wrong."

"I'm fine. Let's just get on with it." I picked my

sword from the training wall, then got into position to parry.

Tisiphone, who had been flying around overhead, fluttered down to the ground near me. "You're not upset because of what happened at the academy yesterday, are you?"

Shaking my head, I considered telling them about my confrontation with Hades, but decided against it. They would think I was whining, and that was one thing the Furies hated above all else: a whiner. They thought it was a sign of weakness to complain.

"Good. Because you should never be sorry for being badass." She chuckled. "I heard you laid out that bitchy girl like that." She snapped her bony fingers.

Caught up in Tisiphone's obvious glee, I couldn't stop the smile blossoming on my face. "She had it coming."

"Of course she did. They all do." She smacked me on the back. "Keep focused and you'll be the greatest warrior the academy has ever seen. Your foes will fear you. They will fear even the thought of you."

"Like us." Megaera dropped down from the ledge she'd been sitting on, landing right beside me and making me jump.

Tisiphone and Megaera smiled at each other while Allecto continued to glower. I'd never seen her smile. She had two facial expressions—glower and scowl.

"Can we spar now?" Allecto twirled her sword

around with her wrist. "I'm getting bored with the chatter."

I raised my sword and faced her. "Bring it."

She did.

Shrieking like a harpy, she attacked, swinging her sword from the right. I dodged and blocked, then thrust at her side. She blocked, danced back a few steps, and brought her sword up and around, aiming for my head. I ducked under her swing, spun around, and kicked her in the side of the leg. When she stumbled and fell, I brought my sword down on top of her. My blade struck the armored cowl around her neck. If that hadn't been there, I would've cut her through.

For the first time since I'd started my training, I got a hit on Allecto.

"Nice!" Tisiphone clapped.

I lifted my sword and took a step back, allowing Allecto up off the floor. She didn't smile, but she gave me an appreciative nod. "Keep channeling that anger. It'll serve you well in the future."

After another hour, I was released from the training arena. I decided that it was the perfect time to test out my helmet. When the bell had woken me up earlier, I noticed my helmet sitting on a table near the fireplace. The note with it simply said: *Use it wisely.*

I decided to take Allecto's advice and channel my anger. I was done worrying about what Hades's motives were and concentrated on mine. Regardless of the reasons why I was here, I needed to find out what happened to Sophie—who did it and why. Those were my reasons.

After showering, I dressed in a sleek black jumpsuit perfect for spy work. I settled my helmet onto my head. An icy chill rushed over my body. I wondered if it was the shadows wrapping around me to make me invisible. Then I walked into a shadow, visualizing the corridor just outside of the dining hall.

Traveling through the shadows was getting easier. It only took me a matter of seconds to get where I wanted to go now. I heard voices inside the hall and walked through the open doors cautiously, still unsure if I was truly invisible. I stood at the front of the room and looked around. No one noticed me. Not even Jasmine, Mia, Georgina, and Ren, who sat at one of the tables together eating dinner, glanced my way.

Smiling, I wandered over to their table to listen to their conversation.

Jasmine snagged a French fry from Mia's plate. "Medic training was tough today."

"Yeah, watching Chiron field dress a pretend amputation of Diego's leg left me feeling sick." Mia pushed her plate away toward Jasmine.

"It was definitely hard," Ren said, "but something we're going to have to face at some point."

"Do you really think we'll have to go into battle?" Mia played with the cap on her water bottle. "I know that's why we're here, but it just seems so impossible."

"I heard Demeter say there have been some grumblings from Tartarus. It sounds like some of the Titans aren't happy," Georgina said.

"But they're locked away. No Titan is getting out," Mia said.

Jasmine and Ren shared a look, and I wondered if they were thinking about the destruction we'd seen when we went to our hometowns. They knew, as well as I did, that those earthquakes weren't normal.

"Mel said that maybe a Titan had been released by someone," Jasmine said.

Mia gave her a look. "I don't think we can trust Melany's word anymore. I mean, she's really changed. She could've killed Revana the other day. That's just not cool, even if Revana's a bitch."

Jasmine, Ren, and Georgina looked at each other but didn't say anything.

I hated that they weren't sticking up for me. Maybe Mia was right, and I'd changed and didn't deserve their loyalty anymore.

I was about to take off my helmet and reveal myself, so we could talk about it, but laughter at the doors got my attention. I turned to see Revana and Lucian walking into the dining hall together. Revana laughed at something Lucian said. Obviously, they were closer than Lucian had let on. Anger instantly swelled inside my belly like a wildfire.

They parted, and Lucian joined the others at the table. He sat beside Ren. "What's on the menu? I'm starving."

My whole body started to shake. I wanted to smack the smile off Lucian's face. Instead, I hit Mia's water bottle, sending it sailing across the table. It landed on Lucian's lap, soaking his pants.

"What the hell?" He jumped up from the table.

Everyone kind of snickered nervously and looked at each other.

I didn't wait to see what the verdict was. I marched across the room and out into the corridor.

I hurried through the academy, my strides long, my fists clenched. I imagined if anyone had seen me, they would've jumped out of the way. As it was, I nearly ran into two people as I rounded the corner into the main foyer.

I stopped and sagged against one of the walls to get myself together. I couldn't walk around here so angry; I was going to do something irrational. Something I'd probably regret in time. I considered taking off my helmet, but when I spotted Aphrodite coming down the corridor, I was glad I hadn't. Here was my chance to follow her.

When she walked past, I got in behind her a few paces. Although I was invisible, I knew that I could still make all kinds of noise, so I employed all I learned from Tisiphone and crept on silent feet behind the Goddess. Once she went around another corner, I knew where she was headed—her hall.

As she approached the tall golden doors, they opened for her as if sensing her presence. I had to bridge the gap between us if I was going to get inside before the doors closed on me. I jogged a little on my tiptoes, so I was maybe four feet behind her.

She sailed through the doors and I followed. For a brief second, her head turned to the right just slightly, and I thought she figured out she was being followed. But she continued on through the golden tiled corridor and into her private rooms.

Once inside, she went to a tall metal stand near one wall. Several crystal decanters of liquid sat on top along with tall crystal glasses. She picked up a pitcher of amber liquid and poured some in two glasses. Obviously, she was expecting company.

I didn't have to wait long to see who that particular company was. Ares strode into the room, wearing the same clothes I'd always seen him in—shorts and a T-shirt. I didn't understand why she was with him; he looked like an angry gym teacher when she was married to a really strong, intelligent man like Hephaistos, who I suspected would do anything for her if she asked. Sure, he wasn't nice to look at, but that couldn't be the only important thing in a relationship, could it?

"Sorry I'm late. Some of those mortals are so weak and whiny. Sometimes, I wonder why I don't just slaughter the lot of them and be done with it." He came to her, and she handed him the glass of liquid. He took a sip.

"Because we need them for now. Like cattle, they're being raised for the impending slaughter."

Startled by her admission, I took a step backward. The bottom of my boot scuffed against the pristine tile. I wasn't sure if I made a sound.

"I heard from Cottus, and he said the release of the chimera would be eminent—"

The air around Aphrodite suddenly blew up, twisting around her, then where she had been standing, now a giant snake sat coiled, ready to spring up any second. It had her golden eyes.

It was my cue to get the hell out of there. But before I could turn to find a shadow to dive into, the snake shot forward and twisted around me. She constricted around me so tightly that I couldn't breathe, and my helmet literally popped off from the pressure she placed on the rest of my body. It clattered to the floor.

Ares's eyes widened at the sight of me. "Well, that's a surprise."

She kept squeezing me tighter and tighter. My bones ground against each other. I heard the cracking noise of my joints as my shoulders dislocated. Pain zipped through me and I cried out.

"Careful, babe. You don't want to make a mess in your nice, clean room."

I squeezed my eyes shut as the pressure mounted in my chest and head. I didn't want my eyes popping out of my head. Then the compression lessened until I was a panting, sobbing, quivering mess on the pristine white tiles. I opened my eyes to see Aphrodite, back in her perfect, pale form, leering down at me.

"How dare you spy on me?! I've killed mortals for less."

I gasped for more breath, hoping it would stop my lungs from burning. It felt like I'd swallowed hot coals. Tears kept rolling down my cheeks as the pain from my dislocated shoulders nearly incapacitated me. I couldn't think beyond the agony.

Ares joined her to loom over me. "What should we do with her?"

"Kill her."

"We can't, you know that. She has Hades's backing. It would be a dangerous move to do that."

"She's invaded my privacy."

Ares gave Aphrodite a gentle pat on the shoulder. "I know, my love, but killing her is not an option." He toed me in the arm with his shoe. A bolt of agony stabbed me in the side and I gasped. "You dislocated her shoulders. It must be extremely painful judging by the tears and the screams. She'll think twice about spying on you again."

That seemed to placate Aphrodite, as she sighed and walked back to the table with her drink on it. She picked up the crystal glass and took a sip. "Fine. But please do something with her; her tears are staining my tile."

Ares crouched and grabbed me around the ankles. He dragged me across the room, out the door of her private chambers, and to the main doors of her hall. When the main doors opened, he proceeded to drag me out.

The pain was constant as I slid along the floor, and there was nothing I could do to stop him. As I passed through, I looked up to see Revana and Eros smirking down at me as I went by their feet. I was in such agony that I couldn't even muster enough concern for it to matter that she saw me like this.

Once outside the main doors, Ares dropped my legs to the ground. "Have a good night." He then left me there like yesterday's trash and returned to the hall. The doors shut behind him.

"Blue. Oh my Gods, Blue!"

I cried harder then as Lucian and Jasmine and Georgina and Ren all gathered around me. I blinked up at them through the veil of tears. My friends had come to save me. I wasn't alone.

Then I passed out.

CHAPTER EIGHTEEN

LUCIAN

"Good Gods, what happened to her?" Georgina crouched next to Melany and checked her pulse. "Her pulse is strong, but she looks and feels feverish."

I got on my hands and knees next to her. "Mel? Can you hear me?" I looked her over, to assess her injuries. Her arms didn't look right. They were lying at an impossible angle. My stomach churned at the thought of what could've happened to her for that kind of injury. "I think her shoulders are dislocated."

"We need to get her to Chiron," Ren said.

"How do we move her?" Jasmine paced the corridor. "What if we make it worse?"

I glanced at Ren; he was the most proficient in

healing than the rest of us. "Can you put her shoulders back? Then I could carry her."

He rubbed his mouth and frowned. "I don't know. What if there is a tear? I could really mess her up."

"Can you try?"

Ren kneeled down next to Melany. He placed his hand gently on her shoulder and moved it around. His brow furrowed as he assessed the damage. Because of his affinity to water, he found that he could sense injuries inside a body because we were made up of sixty percent water. I remembered how surprised he'd been when he learned he could feel inside the body.

He rocked back on his feet. "Yeah, it's just dislocated. I couldn't sense any tears of muscle or tendons."

"What do you need me to do?"

"You'll need to hold her down while I pop it back in."

We made sure she was laid out perfectly straight on her back. While I pressed down on her chest, Ren picked up her right arm and brought it down to almost her side and then gripping her wrist, he pulled it up to a ninety degree angle, shook her arm up and down. Then he held it up to a one hundred and eight degree angle and shook her arm up, then down. I winced when I heard the pop of her shoulder going back in.

With a gasp, her eyes sprang open, and she tried to sit up. I wanted to cradle her in my arms but knew that wouldn't be good for her. So I kept her pressed to the ground, but damn she was strong. She'd gotten stronger over the past few months. "Stay still, Blue. Ren is fixing you up."

She turned her head to look at me; there was a wild look of horror in her eyes, then she sagged into the floor, and her eyes flickered closed again.

Ren met my gaze over her body. "Need to switch positions, so I can do the other arm."

We moved around her, and Ren popped her other shoulder back in. Once that was done, I carefully picked her up into my arms, and as a group we marched through the academy and to the infirmary. If we'd been alone, I would've kissed her face and whispered to her that everything was going to be okay. Even when I wasn't sure it would be.

There were whispers and stares as we passed our peers in the hallways. Mia found us right before we arrived at the infirmary; she said she heard rumors Melany had been injured when she attacked Aphrodite in her private room.

"Bullshit," I said. "I don't believe that for one minute."

"Lu, we did find her outside Aphrodite Hall," Jasmine said, as she linked hands with Mia.

"So, that doesn't prove anything. We don't know why she was there or what happened."

I carried her into the infirmary. Chiron was across the room talking to Dionysus when I placed her on one of the cots. They both hurried over.

"What happened?" Chiron did a quick visual inspection of Melany.

"We're not sure, but we found her on the floor with two dislocated shoulders."

Chiron pressed fingers to her shoulder and then frowned.

"Ren put them back in," I added.

Chiron nodded and then looked at Ren. "Good work."

"Is something else wrong with her?" I noticed some bruising starting to blossom along her jawline.

Chiron pulled down her shirt and inspected her collarbone and sternum. I could see more bruising.

"Looks like she's had lots of trauma on her muscles."

"From what?"

His eyes narrowed. "Not sure, but it almost looks like she's been squeezed in a vice." He straightened and waved his hand at us. "Get out so I can do a thorough exam of her."

"I want to stay," I said.

Dionysus gestured to the door. "Let's all go and have a nice cup of tea. Let Chiron do his thing, and then you can come back. Okay?"

We followed Dionysus out and down the hall to his "office." There was literally no room as we all filed inside. Just about every surface was piled high with books and papers. All the shelves were crammed with herbs and glass bottles of this and that.

He pointed to a sofa that was covered with books and a couple of animal skulls. "Just push that off and sit."

Georgina managed to make some space for us, and the four of them sat while I paced around the room.

"This is Hades' fault." I paced, spun, and paced some more. "He's put her up to something."

"You don't know that, Lucian," Mia said.

"How did you even know she went to Aphrodite's Hall?" Jasmine asked. "How did you know she was here in the academy?"

"I smelled her perfume in the dining hall." I sighed. Her scent was so distinctive to me I'd recognize it anywhere. Like lilac wood smoke. A bit sweet and a lot fiery. "And when the bottle went flying across the room, I didn't think that was magic."

"You think Mel did that?" Georgina frowned.

I shrugged. "I don't know for sure. But she was there in the dining hall when we were talking."

"Why go to Aphrodite?" Mia asked.

"Mel's looking for answers," I said.

"About the earthquake." Jasmine glanced at Ren, who swallowed.

Mia grabbed Jasmine's hand. "Do you really believe her that it wasn't a natural disaster, that someone orchestrated it?"

Jasmine nodded. "I do."

"I do, too," Ren agreed.

"Mel is many things, but a liar isn't one of them," I said.

Dionysus was quiet during our conversation, busying himself making a pot of tea, but I knew he was listening. He reacted a couple of times to what we said.

"What do you think, Dionysus?" I asked.

He shrugged, as he poured tea into four cups. "I try not to." He handed me a cup. "I find it can be extremely dangerous to have opinions."

"How can you be so indifferent? Shit is happening around here."

"My dear boy. I've been around for a few millennia and been involved in several wars. I've seen more bloodshed than you could even imagine. The shit, as you say, that is happening around here is just family politics. It doesn't even raise a blip on my 'this shit matters' radar." He took out a flask from his pocket and tipped it toward me before taking a healthy swallow.

After we finished our tea, we returned to the infirmary, but Chiron would only let one of us in at a time. I didn't even give anyone else a chance to go first. I barged inside, and saw, thankfully, that Melany was awake.

Her smile was soft and hesitant when I pulled up a chair to her bedside. "Hey."

"You're really just going to say 'hey' to me and that's it?"

She shrugged, but I could tell it caused her pain.

"What were you doing at Aphrodite Hall? The rumor is you attacked her."

She smirked. "Let me guess who started that one. Revana?"

I didn't say anything because she was right; it was Revana spreading that story, which made sense, as Aphrodite was her patron.

"Tell me the truth, Blue. Tell me everything."

"Hades believes me about the earthquakes. He suggested that possibly Aphrodite had something to do with it, as she possesses the golden rope of truth. Anyone who wears it will do her bidding." She winced a bit, obviously in more pain than she would ever let on. "Like the piece of golden rope I found where my mother was killed."

"I know you have a… I don't know, a thing for Hades—"

She sputtered. "I don't have anything for him."

There was something in her eyes when she said that, but I didn't want to acknowledge it. Hades had some kind of power over her, and maybe she didn't even realize it. I didn't know for sure.

"But he has his own agenda. They all do."

"I know that." She coughed and winced again, and I helped her adjust the pillow under her head. "Aphrodite and Ares are planning something." She put up her hand to stop me from saying anything. "I was right there when they were talking. I overheard them mention something about releasing a chimera."

That didn't sound good, but maybe there was an explanation.

She continued, "You should've heard what they said about us, about the cadets at the academy. They said we were being raised for the slaughter." She grabbed my hand. "They're planning something big. Something that's going to take us into battle, I'm sure of it."

"Who hurt you? Was it Ares?"

She shook her head. "Aphrodite. She shifted into a giant snake and nearly crushed me to death. I think she would have if Ares hadn't stopped her."

I swallowed and squeezed her hand, but not too tight. I didn't want to hurt her any more than she hurt now. The thought of her pain, of her dying, made my chest throb and my stomach roil. I brought her hand up to my mouth and pressed my lips to the back.

"I'm sorry if I've been——,"

I shook my head. "Nope. Not going to hear it. You don't need to apologize, Blue."

She gave me a sly smile. "Okay."

"We should go see Zeus. He'd listen to you. If they're planning something, it goes against everything Zeus has been working for."

She licked her lips and then nodded. "Okay, but I think you're going to have to carry me."

I grinned. "Any time."

Then she looked at me for a long moment, as if she was searching for the words she wanted to say. She touched my hand. "I wished we hadn't parted that night during the celebration. That we'd…" Her cheeks flushed a little.

I leaned forward and brushed my lips against hers. "Me too. But we'll have our time."

She didn't say anything, just gave me a soft sad smile. My heart clenched in response.

After promising Chiron that we'd come back, I helped Melany to her feet. I slung an arm around her waist and helped her walk out of the infirmary. Jasmine was the only one left outside the doors waiting. The others had returned to their clan halls.

She rushed to Melany's side. "Are you okay?"

"I will be."

"Where are you going? Shouldn't you be resting?"

"I'm taking her to see Zeus. Something is definitely going on, and he needs to know."

We made our way across the academy campus and to the spiraling ramp that led up ten floors to Zeus's Hall. At the top of the highest tower in the academy was where I stayed with others in Zeus's clan, which wasn't too many of us.

At the bottom of the ramp, I looked up. It was going to take a bit for Melany to make it all the way up. I didn't want to wait, so I picked her up in my arms, unfurled my wings, and flew us up to the top.

She laughed when I set her down. "Did you just sweep me off my feet?"

"Yup, looks like."

I wrapped my arm around her again as we walked

down the wide main corridor, which was aglow with golden light shining down from the domed ceiling to Zeus's private chambers. When we reached the prettily painted tall double doors, which seemed to be the norm in the academy, I knocked.

There was a booming, "Come in." Then the doors swung open.

I helped Melany inside.

Zeus stood in the middle of the room, dressed in long, white robes that he often wore. But he wasn't alone. Aphrodite stood beside him. She looked as regal and elegant as she always did, except for her face; it was pinched in anger, and if I wasn't mistaken, worry.

When she saw us, she smiled, and it was like facing a viper with poison dripping from its fangs. "Oh good, I was just talking about you, Melany."

I had to hold Melany back as she charged forward, her face a mask of fury. I'd never seen her like that before. Her face contorted into something vicious and malevolent. The look scared me. And in that moment, she did as well.

CHAPTER NINETEEN

MELANY

"*Y*ou bitch!" I tried to get to her, but Lucian held me back. It was easy, too, as I wasn't in good enough shape to break free of his strong hands. Pain still rippled through me; my entire body ached.

"You see," Aphrodite addressed Zeus, "it's like I told you. She's unhinged. I think all those months with Hades have warped her poor little mind." She touched her face, where now I could see three red scratches marring her cheek. "You see what she did to me. If Ares hadn't been there, who knows what she would've done."

"Melany is not unhinged," Lucian said. "She has

something to tell you Zeus, and I think you should listen to her."

"She's just going to tell you lies—"

Zeus held his hand up toward Aphrodite. "Let the girl speak." He gestured to me. "Go ahead."

"She"—I pointed to the smirking Goddess—"and her lover Ares are planning to release a chimera onto the Earth. They want to start a war."

"Ridiculous." Aphrodite frowned. "Why would we want to do that? There would be no purpose."

"Because you want to take over. You want more power than you have."

She laughed. "Girl, I'm one of the twelve Gods of Olympus. I have more power than you could possibly imagine." She moved toward Zeus, turning her back to me. "I hope you aren't entertaining the lies this girl is spewing."

Zeus looked at me. "Do you have proof of what you're saying?"

"I heard them say it. I was in her room. I was invisible. They didn't know I was there."

Aphrodite swirled around and rolled her eyes. "You were in my room and attacked me. I have a witness to that. You scratched my face. Here's the evidence."

If Lucian hadn't been holding me up, I would've charged across the room and done more than just scratch her face. I'd gouge out her eyes and feed them to Cerberus.

I looked imploringly at Zeus, sure that he could

smell her falsehood just as well as I could. "Aphrodite is a Goddess, and I'm merely a mortal cadet. Do you really think I would be able to injure her like that? She's as quick as a striking snake. There's no way I could even get to her before she crushed me."

Lucian squeezed me around the waist and leaned into my ear. "Good one."

Zeus sighed, looking at Lucian. "Did you see or hear this exchange?"

Lucian quickly glanced at me, and I could see the war of conscience on his face. He was probably the most moral person I knew. When society talked about an innately good person, they were talking about Lucian.

He shook his. "No, but I believe her."

Aphrodite chuckled meanly. "Of course he does. He's in love with her. We all know the things men will do for love."

Zeus stroked his beard and then walked around the room. He went to the huge window along one wall and peered out over the immense academy grounds. "I'm afraid since you have no proof, I'm going to have to side with Aphrodite. Therefore, you will be punished for trespassing in her private chambers and for attacking her."

"That's bullshit!" I pulled away from Lucian this time and was about to cross the room, when a dark mist swirled out from under the doors, twirled up like a mini tornado, and then fell away, leaving Hades standing there, looking fierce and dangerous in a black suit.

"There will be no punishment."

Aphrodite nearly bared her teeth. "You can't just pop in whenever you want and demand things."

"I can and I will." He mounted the steps to where Zeus stood. "Melany was acting on my behalf. She went to Aphrodite's chambers to deliver a message from me. I highly doubt any attack happened. Aphrodite probably scratched her own damn face—her nails are long enough."

Before I did anything else, I listed to the right. Hades zipped over in a flash and caught me before I fell. Lucian had also moved toward me, but Hades had gotten there first.

"I got her, son. You can stand down."

Lucian's hands started to glow as electricity swirled around his fingers.

Hades's eyes turned jet black. "I wouldn't if I were you."

Zeus clapped his hands together sending a crack of thunder through the room. The windows shook. "Enough! All this bickering is giving me a headache."

"If we're done then, I'll be taking my charge with me back to her room, and no punishment will be doled out." He looked me over, seeing that I quivered. He noticed the bruises blossoming along my neck and chest. "It looks to me that Melany has suffered enough. Honestly, if anyone should be charged with a crime, it should be Aphrodite. I'm sure there's some rule or law that states a professor at the academy shall not harm a cadet. And if there isn't, there should be." He clucked his tongue at Zeus. "Just what kind of school are you running here, old man?"

Aphrodite glowered at him. "You are insufferable."

"I'm aware." He nodded to Lucian. "See you later."

Before I could say goodbye to Lucian, Hades touched the amulet hanging around his neck, and we zoomed into the darkness. A few seconds later, Hades half carried me out of the shadows and into my bedroom.

He helped me to my bed and sat me down on the edge of the mattress. "You are a lot of trouble, you know that?"

"I'm aware."

His chuckle sent a pleasant vibration over my body. And I hated that I reacted to it.

"What did she do to you?"

"She shifted into a giant snake and—"

"Yes, I've seen what she's capable of." He took a step back and regarded me. "I'll run you a hot bath. I have some healings salts that Apollo made me. An hour in the water and you'll be good as new."

Before I could reply, he strode into the en suite. Seconds later, I heard the water rushing from the tap. Then he came out.

"It's all ready for you."

"I, uh, I left my helmet in Aphrodite's room…"

He smiled and shook his head. "No, you didn't. It's right over there." He pointed toward the hearth. I leaned forward and looked, and sure enough my helmet sat on the table where he'd put it the night before.

"I made a quick pit stop before floating into Zeus's place. I thought you might need it again sometime."

"They're planning something. Aphrodite and Ares."

He nodded. "Not a surprise. They are schemers, those two. Always have been. The stories I could tell you." His gaze dropped, and he appeared a bit sheepish to my surprise. "Have your bath and I'll make sure Charon prepares your favorite meal." He frowned. "Which is?"

I chuckled softly, touched he was making an effort to make me feel better. I wouldn't presume to think this was some kind of apology for being a dick the other day, but I hoped it was the beginning of one. "Pizza."

His frown deepened and he shuddered. "Pizza? Really? Out of everything in the world you could possibly eat, your favorite thing is pizza."

"My adopted mother Sophie used to make the best pizza."

"Ah." He tapped a finger to his mouth. "Pizza it is. Do you have a preference? If you say pineapple and ham, I'm going to have to drown you in that bathtub."

"Greek, with extra olives and feta."

He tipped his head. "Greek it is." Then he walked out of my room, so I could bathe.

I limped into the bathroom. After stripping off my clothes, I stared at myself in the mirror. I was a hideous collection of scars and bruises. The only parts of my body that weren't currently disfigured were my right breast, my right hip and buttock, and the small patch of skin at the back of my knees. Everywhere else was pretty much a horror show.

Eventually, the bruises would fade, but I'd always be scarred. Looking at myself, I thought I'd gotten used to them, but I think I'd just been avoiding mirrors.

I turned off the tap on the tub, slowly stepping into the steaming water. I sank down into the tub, gripping the sides to keep my head above water. The moment I was completely submerged all my muscles relaxed. Sighing, I leaned my head back, closed my eyes, and let the healing bath do its thing.

I wasn't sure how long I lay there with my eyes closed, but when I heard a noise near the entrance of the en suite, I opened my eyes and sat forward. Hades leaned causally in the doorway, his gaze averted.

My hands came up to cover my breasts. "What the hell are you doing?"

"I've come to wash your hair."

"What? Are you insane? I'm naked for Gods' sake."

He waved his hand toward me, and a layer of dark mist formed over the water, covering me.

I sank back into the tub. "Okay, that's fine, but why are you washing my hair?"

"Because quite frankly, it's dirty." As he strolled across the floor, he rolled up the sleeves of his shirt. He grabbed the wooden footstool from under the sink and set it near the tub, behind my head. Before I could protest some more, he ran his fingers through my hair. Then using a small clay bowl, he dumped water over my head. It sluiced over my face, and I reached up and wiped it from my eyes.

I didn't know what to do. This was the oddest situation I'd ever been in. Not only was it odd, but I found the whole thing... pleasant and surprisingly tender. I didn't have the strength to just jump out of the tub, especially since I'd be naked and exposed, so I just went with it. I mean, when else was a person going to get their hair washed by a God?

I closed my eyes and sighed as he squirted shampoo onto my head and started to massage his hands over my hair. I didn't realize how tense I was until his fingers worked magic along my scalp.

"Why are you doing this?"

"Because I'm a nice guy."

I snickered. "But you're not, really."

"Maybe nice isn't the best descriptor, but I'm not this terrible, monstrous dark God."

"I know you're not."

"I care about... things and... certain people. And I

feel a certain responsibility for you. Your injuries could've been avoided."

"I'm stronger than I look." I opened my eyes, struggling with the urge to turn and look at his face.

"You look pretty strong to me."

My heart picked up a beat, and I was acutely aware my breathing had intensified. I wondered if he noticed. My teeth bit down on my lower lip. It was so hard not to turn around, to look at him, to see his eyes, and to read them. What would he do if I just stood up in the bath, stepped out, and curled into his lap? Gods, I ached to do that so badly I felt it between my thighs.

But I wouldn't succumb to it. Hades was my teacher, my mentor, thousands of years old and a God, and then there was Lucian. I wouldn't hurt him like that. Even if somewhere deep inside, that cold, selfish part of me wanted to.

Instead, I swallowed down my deepest and darkest desire, and rested my neck against the tub as he washed and stroked my hair.

"Tell me one of those stories."

"What?"

"About Aphrodite. You said 'the stories I could tell.' Tell me one."

"Thousands of years ago, she became infatuated with a mortal named Adonis. He was the son of the Princess Myrrha, who actually despised Aphrodite and refused to worship her. Anyway, it got pretty heated between them, and Zeus had to intervene. He turned poor Myrrha into a tree and then Ares transformed into a bull and killed poor Adonis in a jealous rage. It was quite the scandal for decades."

"That's horrible."

"Yup, it certainly is. Then there was this other time…"

For the next hour, as the water ran cold, Hades regaled me with sordid tales of the Gods. It was both informative and entertaining, and by the time he'd finished, my body felt a hundred times better, even if my heart stayed unsure and confused.

CHAPTER TWENTY

MELANY

*a*fter Hades left—it was an awkward kind of departure that had us both bewildered, but I imagined for different reasons—I got out of the bath, dried off, put on my robe, and padded back into my room. The smell of pizza hit me the moment I entered. My stomach growled in anticipation.

I saw a large pie sat on the table by the hearth. I was a bit disappointed Hades wasn't going to join me but I made do. I grabbed a couple of slices, put them on a plate, and took them to my bed, crawling in under the covers. As I devoured the food, I wished I had Netflix to watch, or a few friends that I could text.

In that moment, I was aware of how alone and lonely I was.

The feeling was so bad I almost considered taking the pizza with me and going to find the Furies in the training room to share it with them. I couldn't imagine any of the sisters eating pizza. Their meals probably consisted of baby chicks with their downy feathers still on and freshly caught eel still alive and wriggling.

After eating, I yawned, feeling pretty relaxed, and my body healed. I snuggled down into bed, drawing the blankets up to my chin. I knew I would sleep like the dead.

Except the dead came to see me in my dreams.

In the expanding twilight, I stood alone on a dirt path in a dense forest. I sensed I knew the way to go, so I started to walk deeper into the trees. After walking for some time, the air around me became denser, cloying, as if it grew fingers that brushed along my skin. I shivered but kept walking.

I came to a fork in the path; both ways looked equally daunting. Weeds and flowers grew over both trails, neither of them too visible in the growing darkness. One path curved upward toward the mountains, and the other twisted downward into the deep gorge. I glanced down at my bare feet; they were already covered in dirt and stinging from the cold, so I didn't think it mattered what route I chose..

Before I could choose which trail to take, the sound of breaking branches came from the surrounding brush. I whirled to my right to see Sophie coming out of the trees toward me. Her usually coifed, grey-streaked hair was in disarray; her face was pinched and paler than normal. Her cheeks had black streaks across them, and there was a dusting of ash all over her and her torn dress. Her feet were bare and bleeding.

She reached for me. "Melany..." Her voice was hollow and cracked.

I backed away from her. I didn't want her to touch me. If she did, I was sure I was going to die.

She kept walking toward me, her hand outstretched. I saw that two of her fingers were twisted unnaturally, and her nails had been torn off. "Melany... you must choose..."

"No. Stay away!"

I tried to run back the way I'd come, but there wasn't a path there anymore, just trees, lots of trees and bushes, foliage so thick I couldn't walk through it.

Then she was right in front of me, her face mere inches from mine. Her deformed hand grabbed the front of my shirt, so I couldn't escape. "Choose! Or die!"

Then she burst into flames.

I screamed as her body disintegrated into ash. Flames licked over the grass and trees around me until I stood in the middle of a fiery tornado.

I jerked awake and bolted up in bed. Sweat slicked my face and body. The sheets stuck to my wet skin. My heart pounded painfully in my chest, and I had trouble controlling my breathing. I jumped out of bed and rushed into the bathroom. I vomited into the sink.

I wiped my mouth and saw black streaks on the back of my hand. I looked into the sink. I had retched up ash and soot and charred chunks. At first I didn't know what it was, and then I saw a finger. It was Sophie's hand.

Screaming, I backpedaled away from the sink, tripped over the step stool, and fell onto my ass on the floor. I stayed there until I caught my breath. When I looked at my hand again, it was pale and pink as it normally was. I scrambled to my feet and gazed in the sink. It was empty. No ash, or soot, or Sophie's hand. No vomit, either.

"Gods Mel, you are losing it."

I ran the cold water and stuck my head under the tap. I was wide awake now.

I went back into my bedroom just as the bell clanged.

I got dressed into my training clothes and headed straight to the training arena. The thought of eating made me want to vomit. Allecto, Tisiphone, and Megaera all looked surprised to see me so early.

"Aren't you the eager beaver?" Tisiphone laughed then smacked me in the shoulder. I winced as I was still sore.

We were about to get ready to do some sparring when Hades strode happily into the room.

"Change of plans. There won't be any training today."

"What's going on?" His look of pure glee made me nervous.

"Training is over; it's time for the main event. There's a huge forest fire raging right now, and the government there has asked for help from the academy. I know Zeus is sending out the troops, and you are going with them."

"I'm not sure why you look so happy about that. It's just a fire."

"Is it?" His eyes shone with excitement. "After all that you went through, do you think this is just a fire?"

I frowned. Surely, after what I'd found out, Aphrodite and Ares wouldn't go through with their plans. Not unless they were confident they would get away with it.

"Besides that, I want to see a test of your powers."

"I'm not your weapon."

"Of course you're not." He strode out of the room just as jauntily as he'd entered, calling over his shoulder, "I'll meet you in my library in twenty."

Gone was the man who had treated me tenderly and lovingly last night. In his place was the tactician, the God with a chip on his shoulder and an agenda that I could only hope to guess.

Tisiphone smacked me in the shoulder again. "Remember to always be ready for anything. Have your wings out at all times. You never know when you'll need them."

I turned to go back to my room to pull on my lightly armored jumpsuit.

"Have fun." Megaera finger-waved to me.

After changing, I went into the library as Hades instructed. He was there waiting for me, dressed in his God-like best dark purple suit.

"Ready?" he asked.

I nodded, although nerves fluttered around in my belly. I wasn't sure why I was apprehensive. We were just going to help the local people to fight a fire. Somehow though, it felt like an audition, and I was up for the role of leading lady, although I was sure a lot of people in the academy would cast me as the villain.

In an instant, the shadows swallowed us up. It was a lot easier now to walk through the darkness, but it still made my stomach flip over, like riding a roller coaster. After walking for maybe five minutes, I could see light and hear voices. Then we stepped out into a parking lot where everyone had gathered, demigods, cadets, and firefighters, still a mile out from the actual fire.

The sign just beyond the lot read Victory National Park. I'd come here a couple of times with Sophie for a picnic near the falls. It was an hour drive from Pecunia.

All heads turned at our arrival, including the three or four camera crews and reporters on the scene.

"What are you doing here?" Heracles approached us, but I was sure he addressed Hades, as he looked horrified.

"Just dropping off the kid for play time." Hades

had the nerve to pat me on top of the head. I glared at him, but he ignored me.

"You can't be here, Hades." Heracles looked around as cameras were swung our way and photos were being snapped. "Gods just don't show up and do interviews."

"Why not?" Hades asked. There was a playful arch to his eyebrow.

I looked past Heracles and saw Lucian, Jasmine, Georgina, Ren, and the rest of my peers mobilizing. I noticed that Revana and her cronies were noticeably absent. Leaving the Gods to squabble, I unfurled my wings and lifted into the air, flying over to my friends. Several reporters, mouths agape, filmed me as I gracefully drifted back down to the ground.

"What's the plan?"

"Nice entrance." Jasmine shook her head but she was smiling.

I shrugged. "It was Hades's idea. He has a flair for theatrics."

Lucian came over and hugged me, his face pressed in my neck. "I'm glad you're here," he murmured against my skin.

"Me too." If it had been a different moment, I would've kissed him long and hard, not caring who was watching, especially Hades. But as it was, the moment wasn't right for that, or for lots of things. I promised myself that after we did what we came to do, I was going to grab onto the moment, onto Lucian with both hands and never let him go.

I checked out the familiar faces standing nearby and the lack of some. I'd expected the entirety of the second year class to be present. "Not everyone is here."

"We're basically a test run. Only a few cadets from each clan that have abilities to utilize," Lucian said. "Zeus thought just having a select few to manage this crisis would be enough to show that the academy is doing what he said it would do."

One of the firefighters walked over to us; he had a captain badge stitched on his heavy yellow jacket. "It wasn't my idea to have you here. I think you're going to get in the way, but if you want to help, then do what I tell you."

We all nodded.

"Yes, sir," Lucian said, taking the lead for the group. "There are a few of us who have water powers and can help with the water dumps."

He surveyed our group and didn't look too impressed. "I'm sure our helicopters can handle that…"

Ren stepped out of the group, raising his hands out in front of him. Within seconds he had twin, basket-ball-sized water balls balanced on his palms. He threw them at the surrounding trees, soaking the trunks.

The captain nodded. "Impressive. But we're going to need more water than that, I'm afraid."

"I'm pretty sure a few of us could actually move the

water from the nearby lake and dump it onto the fire," Ren said proudly. "No buckets required."

The captain stared at Ren. "Ah, okay."

Ren gestured to Marek and a couple of others from Poseidon's clan.

"Be safe," I said to him.

"You too." Then he and the others flew into the sky and disappeared behind the treetops.

The captain's eyes were so wide and his head tilted back so far I thought for sure he was going to fall over from shock. It took a minute for him to snap out of it, and then he gestured to the rest of us. "So, what else can you do?"

"Um, I can move the earth." Georgina's voice came from behind me.

He frowned. "Not sure what that means, or how that will help."

She stepped forward, crouched, and placed her hand on the pavement of the parking lot. At first nothing happened, and then the ground beneath us shook a little. Then a crack erupted in the cement, splitting the parking lot, as a ton of soil spilled out of the fissure, like a dirt volcano.

The fire captain had to jump back before a wave of dirt covered his boots. He gaped at her. "Okay, so, I think you would work well with the hotshot team to make firebreaks to stop the fire from spreading." He pointed to a group of firefighters getting ready to jump into a truck. "Go with them, they're getting ready to head in."

"Be safe." I hugged Georgina.

"You too."

She and a few others ran over to the waiting group at the trucks.

The captain glanced at me. "So, what can you do, Twilight?"

I started to balk at what he called me, but as nicknames went, it wasn't bad.

I flicked out my hands to my sides, flames instantly erupting over them.

"We want to stop the fire, not make more," he said.

I shot out a hand, tossing a fireball onto the grass. It immediately took hold and the flames grew. Then I held out my hand toward the fire and slowly made a fist. The flames grew smaller and smaller. Then I shut my hand, and the fire extinguished in a puff of black smoke.

"Can you do that on a large scale?"

I shrugged. "Don't know. Haven't tried to yet. But as a team," I said, glancing at Lucian and Jasmine and the others, "I'm positive we can do something worthwhile."

"All right. I have a team inside about five miles near the gorge. Do you know where that is?"

I nodded.

"I'll radio in, tell them to expect you." He rubbed his face and sighed. "They're not going to believe it when I tell them a group of flying kids are coming to save the day."

With a nod to the others, I lifted into the air, Lucian and Jasmine beside me. The last two, which included Quinn and a girl name Su, who were both in Hephaistos's clan, also followed suit. Once we got into formation, we flew up over the trees. It was then we saw what we were flying into. It resembled the bowels of hell.

CHAPTER TWENTY-ONE

MELANY

*I*t didn't take us long before we were flying through the thick, black smoke. I felt the heat from the fire down below rolling up over my body. Sweat popped out on my forehead and upper lip. I looked over at Lucian and saw the same horror on his face that I was feeling.

Because the air was so thick with blinding smoke, it was difficult to see where the gorge was. After about ten minutes searching, Jasmine pointed out a break in the fire about one hundred feet from the edge of the gorge.

"There!"

We swooped down to the ground where there were about eight firefighters in yellow gear and helmets, digging

in the already burnt ground and knocking down blackened trees to stamp out any embers. When we landed,
there were some startled looks and some curses, but since
they'd been warned of our arrival, it was minimal.

One of the men approached us. "I've been told you
can control fire."

"We're going to try," I said.

"Where do you want us to hit?" Lucian asked.

The firefighter pointed to the fire line to the left of
us. "If we can keep making strides this way, we can
pinch the fire off. From what I've heard, your people
with the water are doing some good damage on the
main fire."

My heart lifted at those words.

The five of us—me, Lucian, Jasmine, Quinn, and
Su—moved toward the fire line on the left. The heat
was oppressive this close to the flames. We were a good
fifty feet away, but it was like putting your face right
into a bonfire.

"Okay, we need to try and gather the fire and snuff
it out."

Everyone nodded. Then as one, we stretched our
hands out toward the flames.

I concentrated on one flame at a time. It was
impossible to think about it all at once. We wouldn't be
able to control it like that. I closed my eyes and focused
on one of the burning trees, trying to gather the fire to
me. But it was hard to distinguish one flame from

another. I needed to get closer. I took a few steps forward.

"Mel! What are you doing? You can't get too close." I heard the worry in Lucian's voice, but I knew what I was doing.

The fire wouldn't hurt me. It was part of me. I glanced over my shoulder to Quinn and Su. They were part of Hephaistos's clan; they were part fire, too. "Move closer. The fire won't hurt you."

They glanced nervously at each other.

"Trust me."

Then Quinn took a couple steps forward; Su followed his lead. Eventually, they got in line with me.

I saw that Lucian and Jasmine were going to follow, but I shook my head. "You stay there. Keep trying to control it from where you are."

I urged Quinn and Su to go with me right to the edge of the fire. I could see the fear on their faces, but there was no time to coddle them. They either trusted in their power or they didn't. I trusted in mine. I felt it surging through me.

Flames bent toward me, flicking fiery fingers at me. I suspected I'd have red skin and singed hair by the time the fire was done with me. It was difficult to breathe this close, so I tried not to gulp in the much-needed air, as it was mostly smoke.

I stretched my hand out toward the flames. I pulled and plucked at the fire until I had a handful, then I crushed it in my fist, snuffing out its life. Now, I had the fire's attention. Bolstered by what they'd seen me do, Quinn and Su both drew out the flames and extinguished them.

It was a long, involved, painful process, but after an hour, we had a football-field sized part of the forest doused. The fire was angry though, and some of the flames tried to leap over us, aided by the sudden gusts of wind. Two small fires erupted behind me and in front of Lucian.

I whirled around to snuff it out, but Lucian used one of his other powers to douse it. He gathered the water molecules from the air and from deep in the ground, creating a mini waterspout. He sent it spinning over the small fires, and they were immediately smothered.

We came back to talk to the firefighters who were extremely grateful for our help, and they told us that the fire was getting under control in other parts of the forest. Ren and Marek had completely put out a hectare to the right of us, and Georgina had single-handedly created another gorge effectively cutting the fire off from jumping into another part of the park. Maybe they would name it after her.

All in all, we'd done one hell of a job. Zeus and the other Gods would be proud. I hoped Hades would be proud, too.

The firefighters shared their water with us, and I used a wet cloth to wipe the soot from my face and hands. I suspected that I'd have a few blisters on my skin by the day's end. It was worth it, though. Together, we'd done a great thing and helped the community.

Taking one of the water bottles, I walked toward the gorge. It was the deepest gorge in the world at sixteen hundred feet and a marvel to see. Luckily, the fire hadn't dived down into the crevasse and burned away all the rich vegetation growing along its rock walls. Lucian and Jasmine joined me.

We stood near the edge, each taking turns drinking the water. I glanced at Lucian and saw he still had soot on his cheek. I reached over and tried to rub it away. He grabbed my hand and held it to his face.

I was happy standing here with him and with Jasmine. It felt like the past three months hadn't happened and I hadn't changed. Maybe there was still hope for me. That I hadn't turned into an angry instrument for Hades. I could just be me. Melany. A girl who had hoped to find a new life at the academy, and found friendship and belonging and maybe love, as well.

I moved closer to Lucian, so he could put his arm around me. As we stood there, a strange thudding sound rose from the gorge.

Jasmine frowned. "What do you think that is?"

"I don't know. Maybe it's one of the helicopters bringing water over—" Lucian's voice trailed off.

The sudden violent rush of air blowing over us cut me off.

A prickling sensation erupted over my scalp as the hairs on the back of my neck lifted.

I knew what was coming.

"Run!" I screamed at Lucian and Jasmine, but it was too late. It was too late to run, too late to do anything.

The chimera rose from the gorge, a monstrous creature, twelve feet in height, with a yellow lion's head and body, a second head of a goat protruded from between its shoulder blades, and large black dragon wings flapped to keep it hovering above us. A hissing sound escaped it as its tail reared around; a tail that was a ten-foot long green snake with four-inch long fangs, dripping venom onto the rocks beneath it.

I heard the shouts and screams from the men behind us, but it was too late for them. There was nowhere for them to run. The beast opened its lion mouth and a stream of fire spewed out, aimed right at the startled and frightened firefighters.

It was their shrieks of pain as they burned that finally knocked me into action.

"In the air!" I shouted, as I shot up above the chimera. I formed a fireball in each hand and flung them at the creature.

One ball smashed into its side, but it did nothing but singe its fur. It dodged the other ball with ease. By this time, Lucian and Jasmine had joined me in the air. Jasmine tossed fire at it as well, while Lucian formed a lightning bolt and hurled it like a spear toward the chimera.

The beast maneuvered out of the way, but only

barely. The tip of the bolt seared the head of the snake. It shrieked and hissed, but it wasn't injured.

We weren't going to win this fight. We were unarmed and outmanned. There were already four or five dead men on the ground, burnt to cinders, and if we didn't do something, that would be our fate as well.

"Keep it distracted!" I shouted to Lucian, as I dropped to the ground.

"Where are you going?"

But I didn't answer; I didn't have time. I ran for the nearest shadow, sinking into it. The trip back to the Underworld took seconds, and I ran out of the darkness in the corridor and into the training arena.

"Help me!" I shouted even as I dashed to the weapons wall and grabbed a sword and back scabbard for myself, a bow and arrows, and a spear. While I grabbed a shield, the Furies jumped down to the floor from the rafters they usually rested on.

"What's going on, princess?" Tisiphone tried to grab my sword.

I smacked her hand away. "The fire was just a diversion. The real threat is a chimera. And I need your help."

Megaera rubbed her hands together. "We haven't fought a chimera in a thousand years."

Tisiphone grabbed a sword. "Finally. We get to have some fun."

Without a word, Allecto armed herself and then took a few extras.

Together, we went back into the corridor. Before we disappeared into the shadows again, I put my fingers in my mouth and whistled. It was a matter of seconds before I heard the thump-thump-thump of very large feet on the stone floor. The doors to the hall burst open and Cerberus trotted inside, his head ducked down, but his tail thudding against the ceiling.

"Want to go for a run, boy?"

His excited panting was all the answer I needed.

All four of us climbed onto his back, and I guided him into the darkness.

When we came out on the other side, the chimera razed the tree line with another stream of fire. Jasmine was on the ground, one of her wings burnt to a crisp. Lucian was still in the air, zipping around the creature and trying to electrocute it, but having no luck.

Su and Quinn attempted to get the other fire-fighters out of harm's way. Quinn picked up one of the men and flew him to safety while Su tended to another's injuries.

Everyone turned toward us as we emerged from the darkness. The Furies were airborne in an instant. And with triple shrieks, they shot toward the chimera. Cerberus charged toward the hovering beast, but it flew up out of his way. He let out a loud, earth-shaking triple bark.

I took to the air, even as I nocked an arrow on my bow. "Get the others out of the forest," I shouted at

Cerberus. He obeyed and ran over to Su and the injured firefighters.

I let the arrow fly at the chimera. It maneuvered out of the way but ended up in Allecto's path. She sliced the creature across the back leg. It let out a roar. I smiled. It was a small victory, but at least I knew the beast wasn't impenetrable and it could bleed.

As I flew toward Lucian, I threw him the spear. He caught it and dove toward the chimera the Furies had circled. I nocked another arrow, aimed at its goat head, and fired. It was confused now, and cornered, and this time it couldn't dodge away. The arrow pierced its left eye socket.

The Furies let out a collective war cry in celebration and then went in for the attack.

The chimera turned its lion head as Tisiphone dove at it. It opened its mouth, blasting fire. She didn't have a chance to duck. Fire caught her wings, burning them to ash. She dropped from the sky.

Allecto swooped after her and was able to catch her before she plummeted into the gorge. Allecto set her down on the ground, and then shot back into the air, twice as angry, twice as determined to bury her sword into the chimera's flank.

"Cut its wings," I shouted.

I wasn't sure if she heard me, but then she swooped under the chimera and veered up, sword tearing through its right wing. The creature banked to the left nearly colliding with Lucian. But he was able to evade it, going into a roll toward the ground. Right before he reached the rocky side of the cavern, he pulled out of his tuck and soared upwards, his wings spread wide.

Gods, he was magnificent. Like a golden eagle, powerful and majestic. I was lucky to have him in my life.

Megaera flew at the chimera's other side, Jasmine with her, and swiped high then low with her sword. Her blade caught the left wing, tearing a hole in the leathery webbing. The beast listed to the side again, and I could see it was having trouble staying aloft.

It was now or never.

Bolstered by seeing Lucian's power in the air, I slung my bow over my shoulder and unsheathed my sword. As I flew upwards, I met his gaze and smiled at him. I knew it wasn't the most appropriate time to feel joy, but I did. It raced through me like the fire raced through the trees. I felt empowered. I felt invincible.

I swooped toward the chimera, avoiding the stream of fire spewing from its mouth. The attack had been desperate, a last ditch effort to kill someone before it fell from the sky. On the ground, the beast wouldn't be as efficient and it knew that.

I dove down, spun, and then came up again. As I shot directly toward the chimera, I feinted to the right, the beast turned to the left, but I whirled at the last second and brought my sword down. I closed my eyes, knowing my blade struck true.

The chimera dropped to the ground, its lion's head

rolling across the blackened landscape. Its blood stained the soil. The body landed with a loud thud. The Furies descended on the beast to finish the job.

I floated down to the ground then looked for Lucian. He was descending slowly near the chimera, a look of triumph on his face. I grinned at him again and he returned it.

Then his body convulsed and he cried out. He flung out a hand toward me, reaching for me to save him.

"Noooo!" I ran toward him, swinging my sword and slicing the snake tail that had struck him in the back in two.

But it was too late. The damage had been done.

Lucian fell the last few feet from the sky.

I caught him before he could hit the rocky edge of the gorge. As gently as I could, I lay him down onto the ground. His body quivered in my arms. I dared not look at his back, knowing full well that the snake's bite had pierced his flesh and shot venom into his body.

He looked up at me, his face paler than I'd ever seen it. "Blue…" He gasped.

I pulled him closer in my arms, rocking him. "Don't talk. Save your energy. It's going to be okay." Tears rolled down my cheeks as I looked around in a panic for help.

The others started to gather around. Allecto, Tisiphone, Megaera. They looked down at us, faces blank.

Jasmine crouched down beside us.

"Help him," I whispered.

She pressed her lips together as tears ran down her face. "I don't know what to do."

I heard more flapping of wings, and others started to land nearby. Ren ran to our side.

He knelt down and touched Lucian's face, which was sallow and slick with sweat. "What happened?"

I opened my mouth to tell him, but the words wouldn't come. I could feel Lucian's body growing cold in my arms.

"The chimera's snake bit him in the back," Jasmine said, her words wobbling.

Without letting Lucian go, I let Ren roll him a bit, so he could examine his back. The look on his face told me everything I needed to know. Everything I would ever know.

I ran my hand over Lucian's face. "It's okay, baby. You're going to be okay."

"Blue…" He lifted his hand and cupped my cheek. "I love you."

I swallowed down my sobs. "Someone help me!"

Then his hand fell away, and he slumped in my arms. Slowly, his eyes fluttered closed.

That was the last thing I remembered before my whole world fell into darkness.

Thank you for reading Demigods Academy Year Two!

Don't miss YEAR THREE.
We hope you enjoyed Melany's adventures and can't wait to share more with you. In the meantime, we would love to read your opinion on Amazon and Goodreads!

Are you #TeamLucian or #TeamHades? Let us know!

Get an EMAIL or SMS ALERT when Kiera Legend and Elisa S. Amore release a new book to be sure you won't miss any of them.

Sign Up to get our EMAILS at:
www.KieraLegend.com
www.ElisaSAmore.com/Vip-List

Sign Up to get our SMS:
Text AMORE to (844) 339 0303
Text LEGEND to (844) 339 0303

ABOUT THE AUTHORS

Kiera Legend writes Urban Fantasy and Paranormal Romance stories that bite. She loves books, movies and Tv-Shows. Her best friends are usually vampires, witches, werewolves and fae. She never hangs out without her little dragon. She especially likes writing kick-ass heroines and strong world-buildings and is excited for all the books that are coming!

Text LEGEND to (844) 339 0303 to don't miss any of them (US only) or sign up at www.kieralegend.com to get an email alert when her next book is out.

FOLLOW KIERA LEGEND:
facebook.com/groups/kieralegend
facebook.com/kieralegend
authorkieralegend@gmail.com

***

Elisa S. Amore is the number-one bestselling author of the paranormal romance saga *Touched*.

Vanity Fair Italy called her "the undisputed queen of romantic fantasy." After the success of Touched, she produced the audio version of the saga featuring Hollywood star Matt Lanter (*90210, Timeless, Star Wars*) and Disney actress Emma Galvin, narrator of *Twilight* and *Divergent*. Elisa is now a full-time writer of young adult fantasy. She's wild about pizza and also loves traveling, which she calls a source of constant inspiration. With her successful series about life and death, Heaven and Hell, she has built a loyal fanbase on social media that continues to grow, and has quickly become a favorite author for thousands of readers in the U.S.

Visit Elisa S. Amore's website and join her List of Readers at www.ElisaSAmore.com

Find Elisa S. Amore on:

facebook.com/eli.amore

instagram.com/eli.amore

amazon.com/Elisa-S-Amore/e/B00J1QZYM8

bookbub.com/authors/elisa-s-amore

twitter.com/ElisaSAmore

Made in the USA
Middletown, DE
25 March 2023

27688722R00135